BETRAYED BY LOVE

Fleur felt the tears start to her eyes. She had a wild impulse to go back on her words, to find Sir Norman and tell him she could not come tonight. She felt she must have one more evening with Jack, just a few more hours in which she would find a little satisfaction, if only a little, in knowing that physically he was close to her—and yet what was the point?

Restlessly, Fleur got to her feet.

"I've got to learn to hate him," she thought, "to hate all men, to dispense with love—forget about it. This petty suffering of mine doesn't really matter."

She stood at the window and looked out over the garden. She was conscious of the tears brimming onto her cheeks, of an aching heart and the quick throbbing of her pulse. The garden was very still and very lovely.

"Please, God, let me find peace here," she prayed.

Pyramid Books

by

BARBARA CARTLAND

Janette

ESCAPE FROM PASSION

Barbara Cartland

PYRAMID BOOKS 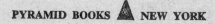 NEW YORK

Pyramid Books are published by Pyramid Publications (Harcourt Brace Jovanovich, Inc.). Its trademarks, consisting of the
word "Pyramid" and the portrayal of a pyramid, are registered
in the United States Patent Office.

Pyramid Publications
(Harcourt Brace Jovanovich, Inc.)
757 Third Avenue, New York, N.Y. 10017

CHAPTER ONE

1942

Fleur came from the room where the Comtesse de Sardou lay dead.

After the heavy, warm atmosphere of the sick-room the air in the passage was chill, but invigorating, like a drink of cold water.

She went to one of the windows and pulled back the thick curtains. Outside in the garden the first rays of a pale sun were dispersing the white ground mist which covered the green lawns.

Fleur sighed, and leant her hot forehead for a moment against the grey stone. There were dark lines of sleeplessness beneath her eyes, but she felt strangely at peace.

Away on the horizon she saw a wisp of black smoke, dark against the hazy blue of the sky. She knew that it was from the destruction of yesterday. All night its fire had glowed fiercely red, the result of R.A.F. machines swooping low over the country early in the afternoon.

She had heard and felt the bombs which had fallen on the factory nearly twenty miles away, a factory in which Frenchmen were turning out hundreds of lorries week after week for the use of their German masters.

The house had shivered and rattled at the impact, but the Comtesse, when she had been told what was happening, had murmured,

"It is good. Only the British can bring us freedom."

"Hush, madame!" Marie had cautioned her. "It is not wise to say such things."

But Fleur had smiled proudly. Yes, it was her countrymen who would bring freedom to the cowed and conquered French nation.

Now, looking at that thick pall of smoke, she thought of Lucien ... thought how too had ridden triumphantly through the skies ... only to fall, as some of those brave men had fallen yesterday, broken and burning to the ground.

At the memory Fleur's eyes filled with tears.

"It is odd," she thought, "at this moment for me to be crying for Lucien and not for his mother."

It had been almost like a stage death, Fleur found herself thinking.

The fine, aristocratic old lady with her white hair and finely chiselled features, a perfect portrait of the *grande dame*, the priest beside her in his vestments, the grave, grey-haired doctor. Marie sobbing audibly at the foot of the bed, canopied and curtained, in which generations of the Sardou family had come into this life and had departed from it.

Yet in the picture, unreal, slightly theatrical, there had been nothing to fear, nothing even of desperate unhappiness and misery.

Only now it was over was Fleur conscious of an immeasurable personal relief. It was as if some part of her had been tense and nerved for something horrible, had shrunk in sensitive anticipation from a terror which had never come.

She had never seen anyone die before and the thought of death was inexpressibly frightening until she found it was nothing more than the closing of the eyes and the folding of the hands.

But death was not always like that. It was not how Lucien had died; yet perhaps for him it was quick and clean—arrested suddenly in the battle, in a moment of triumph.

For they had learnt that he had shot down his enemy,

shot him down in flames, then met a similar fate himself. Lucien—gay, excited, laughing, falling out of the sunlit sky on to the earth of his beloved France.

Fleur stirred and turning from the window went along the passage to her own room.

Even after nearly three years it was hard for her to think of Lucien for any length of time without feeling that agony of physical loss which at first had seemed almost unbearable.

In her own room she bathed her face and started to take off the crumpled frock she had worn all night.

While she was still half-undressed there came a tap at the door. It was Marie. In her hand she held a glass containing some whitish liquid.

"What is that?" Fleur asked.

"Monsieur le Docteur sent it," Marie replied. "You will drink it and sleep. You need sleep, *ma pauvre*—we all do."

Wearily Fleur let her last remaining garments drop to the floor and, slipping over her head the soft silk nightgown which Marie held out for her, climbed into the lavender-scented, hand-embroidered linen.

"Drink this, *ma petite*," Marie said soothingly, and without argument Fleur swallowed the draught.

It tasted slightly gritty and bitter so that she made an involuntary grimace as she handed the empty glass back to Marie, then snuggled down on her pillows.

"I will call you later, Mademoiselle."

Marie pulled the heavy curtains across the open window. The room faded into a grey twilight and she went softly out, shutting the door behind her. Fleur closed her eyes.

It was sheer ecstasy to feel her muscles relax, her limbs sink into the softness of the feather bed. She felt sleep come creeping over her in soft warm waves ... encroaching ... retreating ... each time a little more of her ... consciousness enveloped....

*　　*　　*

7

She awoke suddenly with a start to find Marie standing beside her bed with a tray on which there was a steaming cup of coffee and some biscuits. Fleur rubbed her eyes and sat up.

"I have had a marvellous sleep, Marie. What time is it?"

"Nearly three o'clock."

"As late as that? Oh, you oughtn't to have let me sleep so long."

Marie smiled, her old eyes were swollen from crying but she looked, Fleur thought, happier and less stricken than she had earlier in the day.

"What has been happening?"

"We have taken Madame down to the Chapel. She will lie there tonight and tomorrow—the day after will be interment."

Fleur sat up and put out her hand for the coffee. Then she gave a little exclamation.

"But Marie! This is our best coffee—from our store—and Madame's biscuits!"

"Why not?" Marie asked defiantly. "What are we keeping them for? For those Germans? For those cousins who could not even come to receive her last blessing? No! Eat them, Ma'm'selle; she would like you to have them. For the others—let them enjoy their ersatz."

Marie almost spat the words. Her old hands were trembling.

"We mustn't condemn Madame's relations unheard," Fleur said reprovingly. "Perhaps they could not get here—permits from unoccupied territory are difficult to obtain."

"They have never tried to come," Marie said, "not all this time since M'sieur Lucien has been gone. But now that they are sure that there are pickings, you will see they will gather round like vultures ready for the feast."

"What do you mean?" Fleur asked. "The doctor notified them weeks ago that Madame was ill but there was

8

no reply. Have you heard now that someone is arriving?"

Marie shook her head.

"But they will come all the same," she insisted.

"And only you and I to receive them!" Fleur said, dropping her chin reflectively on her hand. "I shall have to go away, Marie. It is all very well to deceive the Boche, but the family will not be so easily taken in."

"But where will you go, Mademoiselle?"

"I don't know."

Fleur reached out her hand and took one of the sweet biscuits sprinkled with sugar which had been kept specially for Madame all these months of privation.

But although Marie might hide biscuits and brandy and other little delicacies to which Madame had been accustomed she could not hide human beings, and Fleur realised for the first time how dangerous her position was.

The months had gone by like a dream, smoothly and uneventfully. The Germans had come to the house, it was true, but Madame had dealt with them, had made her own explanations, had granted their demands with a cool, dignified disdain more insulting than abuse.

The Château was off the beaten track, they had not been required to billet men or armies, they had not been molested in any way save that a certain part of the farm produce was removed, the car which had belonged to Lucien was taken from the garage and various farm implements were commandeered without explanation or excuse.

Otherwise the ways of the household had continued uninterrupted, except that at the back of their minds there was that fear, unexpressed, but nevertheless as real as if each knew they were being watched by some animal, crouched and waiting to spring.

It was there, always there; never for a moment could one escape it.

Even locked in her own bedroom, two floors up in the Château, and in the middle of the night, Fleur must take a wireless set from its hiding-place, put it under the bedclothes and there listen in.

Sometimes she chided herself for being so careful, yet she knew that it was not cowardice, but a simple realisation that they were surrounded by the enemy, that every wall had ears, that the slightest slip might bring death and destruction not only to herself but to those others who loved and housed her.

"We must think, Marie," she said now. "We must think of something. In the meantime, I will get up and dress."

She finished her coffee, drinking it slowly, savouring every mouthful. It was a long time since she had tasted anything so good. It was delicious. And the biscuits too, how she craved at times for something sweet!

Marie pulled back the curtains and the afternoon sun, hot and golden, came streaming in.

"There have been no aeroplanes this afternoon?"

Marie shook her head.

"None," she replied, "but Fabian came up from the village a little while ago and he told me that those devils got two down yesterday and one fell about ten miles from here in a field. The villagers ran to help, but it was too late. The brave men were burned, all save one, and the Germans took him away to hospital."

"Was he badly hurt?"

"Fabian did not know, but I would rather be in the hands of *le bon Dieu* than at the mercy of those *cochons*."

Fleur swept back the hair from her eyes. For the thousandth time she wondered whether she would have preferred Lucien to have been a prisoner or to have been certain of his safe keeping, as Marie put it, in the hands of *le bon Dieu*.

Stories of the prisoners being hungry and without heat or proper clothing had been whispered over France after the departure of the British Expeditionary Force from Dunkirk. But now—if one could believe such reports—things were better and there was always a chance that the French prisoners might be repatriated.

Yet it was a slender hope, so very few had come back. There was a great deal of talk, a great deal of unquenchable optimism but nothing happened. Perhaps things were best as they were.

But it was hard to be certain when one thought of Lucien, shot down that first fortnight in September 1939, when the world had hardly grasped the fact that hostilities had begun, or that the last war to end all wars which had slaughtered the flower of the European nations had been a failure.

In the first fortnight! Fleur could remember, as vividly as if it was still happening, that moment of incredulous surprise, a moment more of astonishment than of agony, when she had heard that Lucien had been killed flying over the Maginot Line.

It was then that the coldness between herself and Lucien's mother had broken, the barriers had fallen. The two women had wept together, united by an agony of loss as they could never have been had Lucien lived.

Strange now to think how frightened she had been of the Comtesse, yet nothing in Fleur's life had prepared her for someone like Lucien's mother.

Now, at last, she could understand what had seemed to be the mystery surrounding her own French grandmother, after whom she was named, and could realise why her mother had always spoken of her with what amounted to reverence rather than affection.

Aristocrats! It was impossible, Fleur thought, for her or any of her generation ever to emulate the dignity, the poise and the composure of such women.

"We haven't the leisure to be graceful and calm," she thought once. "We have to grasp greedily at everything we want in case someone else gets it first."

That made her think of Sylvia—Sylvia, with her red-painted nails, her red, curving mouth and her bold eyes ... Sylvia, slopping about the house until luncheon-time in a tatered, tawdry dressing-gown and an old pair of slippers with worn down heels ... Sylvia, blowsy,

11

untidy and sometimes dirty, and yet always triumphantly beautiful—beautiful with a lewd lustfulness
which could not be ignored—flamboyant, gaudy and
yet desirable.

Fleur could still shudder at the agony of those days
when her father had first brought Sylvia home. When
she had laughed at the decorations and at treasures
tender with childish memories, when she had turned the
place upside down, filling it with her mocking laughter,
her lip-stained cigarettes and her noisy, rollicking
friends.

Impossible to believe that any man could put such a
woman in her mother's place; and yet, despite all her
antagonism, despite what was a bitter, live hatred, Fleur
could understand a little of her father's besotted infat-
uation.

Everything that was fastidious and decent within herself was revolted by her stepmother, but at the same
time she could not help seeing Sylvia's attractions—the
attractions of an animal, but so obvious that they could
not be ignored.

At first Fleur had been bewildered, had withdrawn
into an antagonistic reserve; and then, when she realized the depth of Sylvia's depravity she stood aghast—
not for herself, but for her father.

It was only slowly that she began to notice and to
understand.

She had met a man who liked her and whom she
brought to her home. She was at first deceived by Sylvia's acceptance of him, the charm with which she en-
tertained him.

Then, when the man himself began to make hesitant
excuses began to avoid her, first shamefacedly and then
self-consciously Fleur realised what had happened.

She could always remember walking out of the house
into a storm of teeming rain, tramping blindly along the
cliffs, a mortal sickness making her oblivious of her surroundings and her soaked clothes.

She stayed on at home because despite all his weaknesses she loved her father. Arthur Garton was a clever man as far as literature was concerned; as regards women he was a fool.

He retired from the family business soon after he was forty-five and settled down to write and to play golf, building himself a house bordering the links at Seaford. He was happy there, looking out over the Downs, writing his books comfortably before his own fireside and trying all the time to improve his handicap.

After Fleur's mother died he might have continued the even tenor of his ways until he was an old man had he not met Sylvia.

Sylvia was looking for someone to pay her bills, someone weak and idealistic like Arthur Garton to give her a roof over her head. It was all too easy. They were married just a month after they had first met and Fleur was told only after the ceremony had taken place.

It was too late then for her to protest, too late for her even to remind her father of the woman who had given him twenty years of her life and who had died loving him. Sylvia saw to that. Sylvia was clever at anticipating danger and at turning it aside before it harmed her.

Yet after four years of being married to Arthur Garton she had grown careless. She underestimated him, underestimated, too, the essential decency of a gentleman. When he found out for certain what he must have suspected for a long time, Arthur Garton went for a long swim early one morning.

It was August; there was nothing unusual in seeing a man leave his clothes in a neat pile on the stony beach at Seaford and strike out into the English Channel.

He left no note behind, no farewells. To the unimaginative world it was an accident. Only Fleur was certain of the truth for it was at least ten years since her father had bathed.

It was just before this happened that she had met Lucien. She had met him when she was staying in London with a school friend.

He had been introduced to her casually, and yet the

13

moment their hands had met and Lucien was bowing with that graceful inimitable inclination of the head which was characteristic of his race, Fleur had known.

She had felt something vivid and alive rise up in her throat, almost threatening to choke her, she had felt as if her eyes were shining like beacons, that the message they carried must convey itself to him.

Perhaps he had felt her fingers tremble, perhaps he too had known in that moment the wonder and beauty of a springing flame which would not be denied.

It was a very short time before they acknowledged their love, before they clung together in ecstasy which was all the more poignant because Lucien was going away. He must return to France. He was an airman; he had come over to England on a mission to the Air Ministry. Now he must return and make his report.

"When shall I see you again?"

"Soon—very, very soon, my darling."

"But when?" she had insisted.

He had shrugged his shoulders, and then tipping back her head had answered her question with kisses.

It was impossible at such a moment to believe that fate could separate them, that they could be apart for long. Lucien had gone away and almost immediately after he left, when she returned to Seaford, her father was drowned.

Fleur had been frantic—so frantic that she had been almost deranged in her anxiety to leave the house which she had once called home—the house which sheltered now the woman she knew was her father's murderess.

She had packed feverishly. Without a word to anyone she had crossed the Channel and gone—white-faced and driven by a need which was almost beyond fear— unannounced to Lucien's home.

And he had been glad to see her. If he had been surprised, as his mother had been, at the unconventionality of it all, he did not show it, his expression and his words bore no trace of reproach.

He had held her close, he had promised that they

should be married, and she had been utterly and completely content, caught up in a rapture that was beyond words.

They had been together exactly twelve hours in the Château before Lucien was recalled. Neither Fleur nor his mother had been perturbed. They had paid little heed to the rumours and troubles of international relations, so that, when France and England declared war on Germany, it came like a bombshell.

Only then did they begin to understand what it was going to mean—to Lucien ... to them. A fortnight after war was declared Lucien de Sardou was killed ...

* * *

Fleur fastened on her wrist-watch and got to her feet. "I am ready, Marie. Let us go downstairs."

"You will come and see Madame?"

"Of course," Fleur answered, her voice softening, "but first I want to pick some flowers—the white roses that she loved."

The young girl and the old woman walked down the passage and as they did so there came the sound of a motor-car approaching the Château up the long gravel drive which was now sadly in need of repair.

They both with one accord stood still. Who was it? Their eyes met and they saw each other's fear. Then Fleur moved towards the window which looked out over the front door. The car slowly encircled the sweep in front of the house.

Instinctively Fleur reached out her hand and took Marie's, her fingers, hard and strong, clung to the older woman's—the car drawing up at the front door belonged unmistakably to the German staff.

They stood there as if paralysed as a uniformed soldier jumped smartly out on to the gravel and opened a door at the back of the car. A figure descended—they could see him distinctly—short and squat, wearing dark civilian clothes.

15

He turned to say a few words to some hidden occupant of the car, and then as he raised his hand they heard his voice ring out—

"Heil Hitler!"

There came the echo—"Heil Hitler!" and from the depths of the Château the clanging of the front-door bell.

CHAPTER TWO

Marie crossed the hall slowly, her feet shuffling over the marble floor; then she fumbled with the bolts and chains of the great door.

Slowly it swung open, its hinges creaking, and the man who was waiting outside in the bright sunshine stepped in purposefully as if he had been impatient at the delay.

"I am Pierre de Sardou."

He spoke with authority and his voice, ringing through the hall, was grating and unpleasant.

"The Comtesse?" he questioned, staring at Marie, half-sheltered behind the door.

"Madame is dead."

"So!"

The man came further into the hall. Fleur, listening, had the strong impression that the announcement held no surprise for him—he had known before he came, she was certain of that. She wondered who could have told him. The doctor? The priest? If so, surely they would have warned her, or at least Marie, that a relation was on the way.

She took stock of Monsieur Pierre de Sardou and was not impressed. He was not so short as he had seemed when she had first viewed him from an upper floor, but he was stocky, inclined to corpulence, and it

17

was difficult to believe that he could be a blood relation of Lucien.

There was nothing aristocratic in his appearance nor in his bearing, for his arrogance and his sharply spoken sentences seemed more assumed than natural.

Then he turned his dark eyes towards her and she had the feeling that he was surprised and unpleasantly so by her presence.

"This is . . . ?" he questioned, speaking to Marie rather than to her.

"La femme de M'sieur Lucien."

Fleur felt her heart beat quicker, but she said nothing, made no movement, only stood and waited, as it were, for events to come to her rather than making any effort to precipitate them.

"His wife!" Monsieur Pierre ejaculated. "But why were we not told? We received no announcement of it when we were informed of his death."

Neither woman replied and abruptly he strode across the floor towards Fleur.

"It is correct, what she says," he asked, "that you are Lucien's wife?"

Fleur took a deep breath, then in a voice which she hardly recognised as her own she lied—

"Yes, I am Lucien's wife."

"Madame!" She felt her hand taken and raised to Monsieur Pierre's lips.

Now he was speaking suavely. "You must forgive my surprise. I had no idea. I believed that my aunt, the Comtesse, was living here alone with her servants, but I realise I was mistaken. And are there—you will forgive me asking?—are there children of your marriage?"

Fleur had a sudden insane desire to strike him in the face. She did not know why; it was just that there was something in his smile and the expression in his eyes that made her not only resent his questions but feel afraid of them.

The moment was too chaotic and too unexpected for

her to remain cool, but she was certain of one thing, if of one thing only, that there was danger in every word she uttered, that this man was her enemy.

"I have no child." She spoke quietly. "But won't you come in to the Salon? You would like something after your journey—a cup of coffee, perhaps?"

"I thank you, but I have not long finished luncheon."

Fleur led the way into the Salon. As she opened the door she caught sight of Marie's face and knew by her expression that she was warning her, that she too had sensed danger.

The afternoon sun shining through the lowered venetian blinds made stripes of gold across the Aubusson carpet—stripes reminiscent of bars—prison bars.

"You have been here long?"

"A long time."

"I cannot understand my dear aunt not acquainting me of so interesting an event as Lucien's marriage. Besides, I should have liked to commemorate it with a gift."

"We were married only a short time before he was killed," Fleur said through stiff lips.

"That accounts for it, of course. The shock . . . the unhappiness must have been terrible. And yet courageously she answered her letters of condolence—I received one myself. She spoke proudly and at some length of Lucien—strange that she should not have mentioned his wife. She must have forgotten—that, of course, is the explanation, but it is strange, Madame, you must agree. My aunt was most punctilious in these matters as you may have noticed. When did she die?"

"This morning at half-past six. Would you like to see her?"

"There is plenty of time for that. I shall be staying here tonight, of course. The funeral will be tomorrow?"

"The next day."

"So. Then we shall have the pleasure of each other's company until Wednesday. Perhaps other members of the family may turn up, I do not know, but I myself will

19

have a great deal to do. You understand, I am now the head of the family."

"Indeed?"

"Yes. Of course I am entitled to call myself the Comte de Sardou, but we of the younger generation are not concerned with such trifles—the gaudy baubles left over from an effete aristocracy. No, no, I prefer to be Monsieur. I am a democrat, as I am sure you are, Madame?"

"Of course."

"I am delighted to hear it. We shall have much in common, I can see that. You have seen the will of Madame la Comtesse?"

The last question was shot at Fleur. She took her time to answer, stooping to arrange some small china snuff-boxes on a table, amused to keep her inquisitor on tenterhooks, knowing that here lay the crux of the whole situation.

"No, I know nothing about it," she said at length. "If she has made one it will be with the advocate."

"Of course."

She heard the quick breath of relief which Monsieur Pierre drew. He walked a few paces across the room, then back again.

"May I smoke, Madame?"

"Of course—please do. I am sorry I forgot to suggest it."

"That comes of being in a manless household for so long." He lit a cigarette. "You were here when Lucien was killed?"

"Yes, I was here."

"Where were you married?"

Fleur felt herself tremble. This was the question of which she had been afraid. It was only a matter of time now before she was discovered.

"In Paris."

"At Notre Dame?"

"No, at the Madeleine." She did not know why she contradicted him save for the pleasure of it.

20

"Strange indeed! All the de Sardous have been married at Notre Dame."

"Lucien wished to be the exception."

"You will forgive me, Madame, if I ask your maiden name?"

Fleur smiled. She was on safe ground now, no need to lie. She could give her grandmother's, they were a large family.

"Fleur de Malmont."

"But of course—I know the family."

There was a note of respect now in the suave voice, yet Fleur knew he was by no means satisfied. He was still suspicious, perhaps even more so than he had been before.

Too late she realised the only possible explanation for a secret marriage might have lain in the fact that Lucien had chosen a nobody, a girl of doubtful antecedents whom the family would not have accepted.

Well, it was done now and there was nothing she could do but wait for the next question. Then gladly she heard the sound of the door opening. Here, for a moment at any rate, was a respite.

It was Marie with coffee, or rather the horrible ersatz substitute which was all they had been able to purchase for over a year.

"Coffee, M'sieur?"

"Thank you. If you will put it down I will help myself in a few moments."

Fleur fancied that his nose wrinkled at the smell. Doubtless Monsieur Pierre with his German friends had ways of procuring more palatable beverages than his less fortunate countrymen.

Marie turned to leave the room. As she reached the door he spoke to her sharply.

"I wish to send to the village. Is there anyone who can go?"

"*Mais non, M'sieur*. There is only myself and Madame here in the house."

"But that is ridiculous! A garden boy, perhaps—a man from the farm?"

"No one, M'sieur, to whom we can give orders. Before the war there were many who were glad to serve at the Château. Now they serve our conquerors."

Monsieur Pierre gave an exclamation of annoyance.

"I must go myself, then. I have to see the priest, the doctor . . ." He stopped.

'And the advocate,' Fleur added for him in her mind.

"Yes, M'sieur." Marie stood patiently waiting, stolidly uncommunicative and unhelpful.

"You can go."

"Thank you, M'sieur."

"She is telling the truth, of course," he said, turning to Fleur. "There is no one I can send, no other way of telling such people to come here to me?"

"I am afraid not," Fleur said deprecatingly, "and naturally we have no conveyance."

"Naturally. The car . . . ?"

"The Germans took it over a year ago."

"Yes, of course. They reimbursed Madame for its value?"

"I have no idea."

Fleur knew quite well that the Comtesse had received no recompense for the removal of Lucien's car. She had been told vaguely that if she applied she might be given a voucher for it which in time would entitle her to claim its value. She had done nothing in the matter.

Fleur was determined now that no word of hers should enable Monsieur Pierre to benefit from what had been Lucien's.

"Well, I must go myself—Mahomet to the mountain!" he laughed with an effort. "Au revoir, Madame, I shall not be long. We will dine together, I hope?"

"What time would suit you, Monsieur?"

"Seven o'clock would be convenient?"

"Perfectly."

"Very well, then. Until then, Madame."

He gave her a glance which Fleur realised was meant to be gallant, then left the room with a swagger, as one who imagines that a woman is admiring him.

Fleur stood very still. She waited until she heard the front door close ... until the footsteps scrunching on the gravel came fainter and fainter ... until there was only silence. Then she sank down on the sofa and put her hands over her aching forehead. Slowly she felt her tension relax.

"I must think," she said out loud. "I must think."

What was she to do? How could she escape from the trap which she felt slowly closing round her? Why had Marie said that she was Lucien's wife? It was madness—and yet what else could she have said?

He might have asked to see her papers and then any subterfuge, any other lie might have made him more suspicious than he was already.

How had she been so crazy, she wondered, not to have anticipated all this, to have gone away before; and yet she knew it would have been impossible for her to leave the Comtesse while she was dying.

She had loved the old lady, had been afraid of her, had not understood her—how could she understand someone of another type of life, of another nationality? But she had been her last link with Lucien and Fleur had clung to that, happy in the mere fact of being in his home.

Yes, it had been impossible to leave, impossible to go and forsake all these things which had meant so much; yet now she saw the danger.

The ability of the Comtesse to arrange certain matters had rested on her own personal influence—on the power she exerted in the village traditionally because of her position. Now her place would be taken by another and a very different personality—Monsieur Pierre.

Fleur had often smiled at the memory of the Mayor coming up to the Château at the Comtesse's command. However much France boasted of democracy, in these

23

outlying villages the aristocrats still had their importance, still had their place in the local hierarchy.

The Comtesse requested his presence and the little man, a grocer by trade, came apprehensively into the Salon where Madame was waiting for him. He was sweating a little, Fleur noticed, and he turned his hat round and round in his hands as he listened to what Madame had to say.

"Monsieur le Maire, our beloved country has been invaded once again by barbarians. Once again our soil is violated and the blood of our countrymen cries out for vengeance. You agree, Monsieur le Maire?"

"Yes, Madame—but Madame will pardon me if I suggest that she does not speak of such things quite so loudly."

The Comtesse had smiled.

"I am an old woman, Monsieur le Maire, and I can only die once. My son has already given his life for France—I should be proud to offer mine in the same cause."

"Madame is brave."

Nevertheless, as if he spoke them out loud, Fleur had guessed his thoughts were of himself, of his large fat wife to whom rumour had it he was consistently unfaithful, and of his six children, the eldest of whom was a prisoner in Germany.

"We understand each other," the Comtesse went on. "There is no need for me to say more. But Monsieur, in my anxiety to speak of politics I have omitted to present you to my daughter-in-law, Fleur—Monsieur le Maire—Madame Lucien de Sardou."

Just for a moment the little man had looked surprised and then with the quickness of his race he understood.

"*Enchanté,* Madame, my felicitations," he had murmured, and then he had waited, understanding now what was expected of him.

"My daughter-in-law," the Comtesse continued, "his had an unfortunate accident, Monsieur. A little fire oc-

24

curred here last night, nothing very serious, we were able to put it out ourselves, but most unfortunately Madame's papers were burned, her *carte d'identité*. There is nothing left and, still more unfortunate, no one had thought to take the numbers."

"I understand. Madame—they can be replaced."

"Thank you, Monsieur le Maire, it is most agreeable of you."

The Comtesse had held out her hand, the Mayor had bowed over it and the interview was at an end.

The following morning his second son, Fabian, had arrived on a bicycle. An identification card with her new name. the date of issue mysteriously smudged, had been handed over.

Yet now Fleur saw the pitfalls of what had seemed an easy subterfuge. Most of all she regretted that the Comtesse had made her burn her British passport.

"It is dangerous." Madame had insisted, and despite all Fleur's protestations the flames, real ones this time, had licked greedily round the blue canvas cover and the page which held the Foreign Secretary's name.

Yet how right the Comtesse had been! The next day the Germans had arrived. Marie, a scared look on her usually placid face, had fetched the Comtesse and Fleur from the garden.

"Madame! *Nom de Dieu*! excuse me, Madame, but there are Germans at the door."

She was panting, the frilled cap she wore askew on her grey hair.

"Germans?"

"Yes, Madame. They wish to speak to you."

"Thank you, Marie. You will be calm, Marie."

"*Oui,* Madame."

"And your cap is crooked, Marie."

"*Oui,* Madame."

The Germans searched the house. They looked in every nook and cranny for French soldiers. They took away the pigs and chickens, and a side of bacon which had been hanging in Marie's kitchen. They drained the petrol from the car standing in the garage and made a note to send later for the car itself.

They came again a few days later and took away Louis, the man who worked in the garden; no one was told why. At first they did not know whether the Château and the village would be in occupied or unoccupied territory.

They did not talk about it, but Fleur guessed that the Comtesse prayed that they might be favoured in the little grey Chapel where the flags captured by de Sardous in battle hung above the altar.

One day they learnt that the line had been drawn, they were some twenty miles inside German-occupied France.

Fleur got up suddenly and walked to the window. The garden was quiet and peaceful.

Strange to think that there was terror and brutality over the whole continent, men being shot and imprisoned, concentration camps where those who entered them were beaten into insensibility or tortured until they died or became insane.

Fear and misery everywhere, panic and sorrow, privation and sheer sadism.

"Oh, God, I'm afraid!" Fleur thought to herself.

Then she knew that somehow, in some way, she could and would escape.

CHAPTER THREE

Something was happening ... something was frightening her. Fleur stirred convulsively and tried to scream. Even as she did so a hand was pressed down over her mouth. She experienced a moment of sheer terror ... then she heard Marie's voice.

"It is all right, Ma'm'selle, it is I—Marie. Do not be afraid."

"Marie!"

Fleur turned over, the terror of her dream still with her so that she could feel her heart beating too quickly and her breath coming pantingly through lips that still felt the imprint of Marie's fingers.

"Hush! We must be very quiet. I have news for you."

Fleur sat up in bed. There was a candle by the bedside but its flickering light illuminated only a portion of the room; the rest was sombre and menacing in shadow.

"What is it?"

Marie came very near her, their faces almost touching.

"Fabian has brought information. You must leave at once, Ma'm'selle, you are in danger."

"Tell me—what did he say?"

Marie came a shade nearer and her voice dropped even lower so that Fleur must strain her ears to hear what was said.

"It is Monsieur Pierre. When he went to the village, he went not only to see the priest and the doctor, but also to telephone—to telephone to Paris about you, Ma'm'selle!"

Marie paused dramatically, as one who has reached the climax of her story.

"About my marriage!"

Marie nodded.

"Yes. He spoke to a friend of his, in some office I think Fabian said it was, and he told him to go to the Madeleine first thing this morning and make inquiries as to whether you and M'sieur Lucien had been married there, and gave him approximate dates. He was in a hurry.

"At first, Fabian said, he commanded his friend to go at once, that very moment; but there was some difficulty, the priest in charge of the Register would not be there. Anyway, he is to inquire this morning. That, Ma'm'selle, is why you must go."

"And when he does not find it," Fleur said reflectively, "what then?"

"Then Monsieur Pierre will discover other things. Oh, Ma'm'selle, I was listening last night at dinner when he talked to you. You speak beautiful French, but it is not quite good enough to deceive a Frenchman. A German, yes—what would they know of our language? But Monsieur Pierre—he knows better. I could see the way he was watching you, the way he was listening. Ma'm'selle, he suspects your nationality!"

"And if he does, would he dare to give me up—to denounce me after his aunt had sheltered me all these months? Surely . . ."

"Monsieur Pierre is a traitor to our country," Marie interrupted. "He is working with the Germans, he would be glad to curry favour with them. He is of the type of Laval, that one, and do you suppose that family pride would matter to him more than his personal advantage? No, no, Ma'm'selle, a man who would betray France would certainly not hesitate to betray the honour of his family. You are in danger, *ma petite;* you must go."

"But where? Where can I go?" Fleur made a helpless gesture with her hands.

"I have thought of all that," Marie replied, "and M'sieur le Maire is not without ideas. He told Fabian that those papers you already carry must be destroyed. It is not safe for you to show them to someone like Monsieur Pierre."

"But what will he give me instead?" Fleur questioned.

"I have arranged that," Marie replied. "*Ecoutez,* Ma'm'selle, listen to me. I have a brother—Jacques. He is fond of me and I of him, although I have not seen him for many years. He lives at Ste-Madeleine-de-Beauchamps, a little village not far from Dieppe.

"Jacques had a farm there; it is my home, you understand. Some of his children work with him on the land and some are fishermen. He has a large family. You will go to him with papers from which anyone who reads them will learn that you are his niece."

"But, Marie, how do I know that he will accept me?"

"He will accept you because I sent you," Marie replied. "He has no love for the Germans—his eldest boy, François, was killed fighting in the Ardennes. The Padre wrote and told me of his death for Jacques cannot write. He has worked too hard all his life to have time for learning."

"But supposing . . ."

"Now don't worry, Ma'm'selle. It will be all right, I promise you."

"Oh, Marie—come with me!"

"I have thought of that," Marie replied, "but it would not be wise. If Monsieur Pierre was to look for us he might suspect that I would go home; but for you—no, it will not be so easy. He will have to guess in what direction you have gone."

"But the permit to travel?"

"That is all being arranged for. Fabian has gone back

to his father to ask for them to be made out in the name of Jeanne Bouvais. He will explain exactly to Monsieur le Marie what is required. He will understand—he is no fool, that man."

"It is dangerous for him too," Fleur said. "I don't know why he should do this for me?"

"He does it not so much for you, Ma'm'selle, as to be against the Germans. He may look like a mouse, but he has the heart of a lion."

"I had no idea."

"Nor have the Germans," Marie replied grimly. "He is small and appears frightened and so they let him remain in office; they give him his orders and they are pleased by the respectful, humble way in which he promises to obey them. But they don't know!

"The other day they brought a large train full of produce into our station—produce stolen from our farms, from our gardens, and being taken into Germany. The trucks were not running smoothly and they sent for Monsieur le Maire and told him that ten men were to be put to work immediately to grease the axle-wheels. Monsieur agreed.

" 'And no nonsense, mind,' they added. 'If any man is caught putting sand or anything else into the wheels he will be shot, also his family and those who are working with him.'

" 'We understand,' M'sieur le Maire answered, and he called the men and told them in front of the Germans how important the job was and how well it was to be done.

" 'You must be very careful, *mes enfants,*' he said, 'to see your hands are clean while you are doing this work. If you touch anything save the axle grease, you must go at once to the little stream beside the station and wash.'

"The Germans nodded approval, but those who were listening almost laughed aloud. For that little stream in which they were to wash their hands is the one place in our village where there is sand—good, strong, gritty sand.

"The men understood, of course, and while they were doing their task they obeyed his instructions and ran often to wash. That train carried into Germany many handfuls of our good, strong sand!

"Yes, M'sieur le Maire is not so simple as he looks. You can trust him. But now, Ma'm'selle, we must hurry. You must leave as soon as it is dawn."

Fleur got out of bed.

"What time is it?" she asked.

"Nearly four o'clock," Marie replied. "And look!—I have got your luggage and your clothes ready for you."

She raised her candle and pointed to a dark bundle in the corner of the room. Beside it was a wicker basket and an old dilapidated carpet bag such as the peasants in France invariably carrying when they are travelling, a relic handed down from generation to generation.

"But the clothes!" Fleur said wonderingly.

"Ma'm'selle will excuse them being my own," Marie answered. "I had them many years ago."

There was a note of wistfulness in her voice; and then, as Fleur picked up the dress and looked at it closely, she saw that it was almost new, old-fashioned but trimly tailored, of the heavy black material which Marie still wore on Sundays and in which the majority of women in the village went to Mass.

"But, Marie, I can't take this—your best dress."

"It is too small for me now, I have never worn it very much."

"Why not?"

"It was part of my trousseau."

"And you never married? What happened?"

"It is a long story," Marie said quickly. "We have no time for it now. Come, Ma'm'selle, you must dress."

There was a hint of tragedy somehow, Fleur felt, in all this, and yet she realised that Marie was right. This was not the time to gossip if she was to get away from the Château before Monsieur Pierre was awake.

I must go on the earliest train—the market train, she

31

thought to herself. The one which leaves about five-thirty.

She felt strange when she looked at herself in the glass. Marie had helped her button the tight bodice down the front, caught the voluminous skirt round her waist over several petticoats.

Then she had dragged her hair off her forehead and her ears and covered it with a plain black straw hat. She looked surprisingly young and at the same time unobtrusive—a young peasant girl who might be setting off to take her first situation as a *femme de chambre*.

"Your nails, Ma'm'selle," Marie said insistently.

Fleur looked down at them and understood. They were certainly not in keeping with the character.

All the time she was dressing, Marie was putting her clothes tidily and neatly into the wicker basket and carpet bag. At last she was ready.

"How will you explain my departure to Monsieur Pierre?"

Marie shrugged her shoulders with a kind of fatalism.

"He will blame you," Fleur said. "I cannot have that, Marie."

"Could you leave him a letter?"

"Yes, that is a good idea. I will say I received a telegram that one of my family is ill. I will not say which one or where. No, that would get Monsieur le Maire into trouble. A telephone call is better. He can say he thought it came from Paris."

Fleur went to the writing-table and sitting down wrote a short note.

"*Monsieur,*" she began simply, determined not to stoop even to politeness where such a man was concerned. "*I have received the sad news that my cousin is indisposed. I must go to her at once and do not wish to disturb you. I am desolated that I shall not be present at the interment, but my thoughts and prayers will be with Madame.*"

She did not sign it; she felt that she would not stoop to that last lie, having told so many, She would not assume, not even for the last time, Lucien's name to which she had never been entitled.

She slipped the note into an envelope and addressed it.

"I will not give it to him," Marie said, "until late in the day."

"Be careful, Marie. You must not annoy him more than is necessary."

"I am not afraid. I am old—what does it matter what happens to me? But you are young."

They heard the clock in the hall chime the hour.

"You must go," Marie said. "Fabian will be waiting for you in the back drive. He will give you your papers, and now, Ma'm'selle, there is one thing more."

She drew from her packet a leather bag. As she put it into Fleur's hand it clinked, and Fleur, feeling the heaviness of it, knew that she held coin.

"What is it?"

"It was Madame's," Marie replied. "Always she insisted that we keep a little nest-egg in the house. She could remember so well the invasion of 1870, she knew what happened to the franc in the last war. 'We will have gold, Marie,' she said to me over and over again. 'There is always value in gold.' And so we have hidden it, she and I, but now is the moment to use our treasure, to prove its value."

"But, Marie, I can't take this."

"It is yours because you loved M'sieur Lucien and he loved you," Marie said simply, and all the protestations that Fleur would have made died on her lips.

She knew that Marie wanted her to have this money, that she believed it was her right, and somehow the mere fact of its value was unimportant. It was Marie's wish. No need to suggest that she should have it herself. How easy it would have been for her to take it.

Impulsively, Fleur bent forward and kissed the wrinkled cheek.

"Thank you, Marie. I shall think of it as something coming from Lucien. Perhaps it will help and protect me even as I feel he will help and protect me while I take this journey."

"We are all in the hands of God," Marie answered.

Then for a moment she held Fleur close. Fleur knew then that she was saying good-bye to Lucien.

*   *   *

Trudging down the drive holding her wicker basket in one hand and the carpet bag in the other, conscious of her voluminous shirts and sensible, flat-heeled shoes, Fleur felt as if everything she had known since war began had been a dream.

She saw Fabian standing under the trees. He came towards her and as he lifted the wicker basket from her hands, she turned and looked back at the Château.

A picture from the past, Fleur thought; and already it has passed—passed and gone as far as I am concerned.

She did not know why she was not deeply saddened at the thought, she felt there should be tears in her eyes, that she should feel acutely the drama of the moment.

Instead, as she walked along beside Fabian, she found herself responding to his boyish air of excitement. He thought it was all a fine joke; he envied her, he said, setting off to see a bit of the country.

"It won't be exactly enjoyable," Fleur said, half-reproachful that he should not realise the danger of what she was doing.

"It is always enjoyable to deceive the Boche," he laughed. "I have your permits here, Ma'm'selle. Before we get to the station I will give them to you. My father had an idea. The first paper I shall give you is just a permit to visit Bugalé for the market. That is all you will be asked for this morning. Then, when you change your train, you produce your new papers. There will then be no one there to be suspicious. Here at the station they might think it strange that you should want to go so far."

"I understand," Fleur said, "and will you thank your

father? Will you tell him how grateful I am? I am only afraid that he might get into trouble."

"Father will see that he doesn't do that. You are lucky that he had these permits, Ma'm'selle. He got them from a German who had too much to drink one night. Just as he was going to bed, Father asked him for the usual permits to visit the market the following day.

" 'Find them and I will sign them," the German officer said—he was in a good humour.

"Father took him at his word. He found not only the market permits, but others as well. They have come in very useful one way or another. But naturally, Father doesn't use them except in an emergency."

"He is wise."

"The wisdom of a serpent!" the boy boasted.

They were approaching the station. Fabian stopped in the shade of a haystack and produced the papers. Fleur put them into the old, worn leather purse which Marie had given her and thrust it deep into the slit pocket in her skirt.

It felt strange not to be carrying a bag, but Marie would not let her take one.

"A purse is more usual," she had insisted. "You mustn't make yourself conspicuous."

Fleur had understood. She only hoped that some inquisitive German would not insist on inspecting her luggage; that would give her away quicker than anything.

The platform was crowded with people. Outwardly they looked very like the ordinary pre-war crowd of marketers going off to sell and purchase in the neighbouring town. Only on closer inspection did one realise how terribly little they had to sell.

The big baskets which before the war would have held half a dozen fat ducks, pounds of golden butter and several score of large brown eggs were now pitiably empty. And every owner of such goods wearing an anxious, worried expression as if the expedition was of desperate importance.

There was none of the jolly chatter, exchange of gossip and of cordialities which had been characteristic of the market train. Now passengers stood silent, their shoulders drooping, a weary people for whom travelling was no longer an adventure, but rather an inescapable imposition.

Fabian said good-bye to Fleur before she entered the station.

"Go up to the front of the train, Ma'm'selle," he advised. "There are less people on that part of the platform."

"I will do that," Fleur replied, "and thank you again."

She tried to tip him, taking a twenty-franc note from her purse, but he refused it with a roughness which made him almost brusque.

"You will want it, Ma'm'selle," he said, and then added with a sudden boyish seriousness, "we have not forgotten Monsieur Lucien—none of us in the village."

Fleur felt the tears spring. She could not answer; instead, she turned swiftly away and went into the station.

Her permit was scrutinised and passed back to her; she walked down the platform self-consciously, feeling that eyes followed her. But they were tired eyes, almost too apathetic to be curious.

The train came in belching foul-smelling black smoke which came, Fleur had been told, from using the worst coal. The best had been taken away, taken into Germany to be used in the Nazi war effort. All that was left for the French was what was thrown out, difficult to handle and filthy in use.

The carriage in which Fleur found herself was not full. Her fellow-passengers were an old woman carrying a covered basket over her arm and holding the hand of a small child, obviously her grand-daughter; a workman who smoked a pipe, the fumes from which filled the carriage with an unpleasant acrid odour. A nun, white-coifed and quietly unobtrusive, who sat telling her beads in a corner, never raising her eyes to the faces of the other occupants.

36

After a time the child broke the silence.

"Grand'mère, j'ai faim."

Her grandmother bent down and spoke in a low voice. Fleur heard something about trying to get some food later.

"But I'm hungry now," the child insisted. "I have a hunger here." She patted her small tummy.

The grandmother spoke sharply. The child was quiet, but her lips moved and Fleur saw that over and over again she was saying to herself,

"I'm hungry. I have a hunger."

"They reached Bugalé and it was a relief to step out of the carriage and get away from that oppressive silence of people sitting, thinking, feeling, side by side with one another and yet all too frightened to exchange even a commonplace courtesy among themselves.

After Bugalé, Fleur journeyed interminably, uncomfortably, in silence and for hours. There were innumerable changes, there were, too, many alterations to be made in the ticket, extra francs to be paid.

It was impossible not to realise how deeply France was suffering beneath the yoke of the conqueror. One had only to look out of the window at crumbling walls, the lack of paint, unrepaired gates and fences.

There were, too, more obvious signs; cows with their ribs distinct against their sides; horses which looked as if it was impossible for them to pull even the lightest load; pigs, undersized and in need of fattening; and above all, a shortage of livestock.

Where were the herds which had filled the green pastureland leading down to the winding rivers? Why did the farms as one passed by them appear empty save, perhaps for some mongrel dog, pitably thin, dragging its way from the sunshine to the shade of a tree or bush?

It is a sad land, Fleur thought, and felt her heart contract with the pity of it.

The only cars on the roads were German military vehicles speeding along, often flanked by outriders on motor-cycles, and everywhere they appeared there was the swastika, arrogant, dark and sinister.

The Germans looked well-fed, especially in contrast to the French men and women toiling in the fields.

No wonder that they are hated! Fleur thought. She remembered stories the previous year of crops being snatched away as soon as they were garnered, of whole families being left with little or nothing to eat when the potato crop had been commandeered.

There was a German aeroplane in the sky, moving slowly against a cloudless blue—so had Lucien soared once . . .

On, on she went, the wheels of the train in which she travelled turning monotonously over and over, appropriate accompaniment to the question in her mind, relentlessly insistent—

"After I get there . . . what then?"

CHAPTER FOUR

Fleur stood outside the little railway station and looked about her in a dazed manner. She was so utterly weary that it was difficult to realise that she had really reached her journey's end.

In the distance she could see the sea, shining a dazzling blue in the afternoon sun. Seagulls, squawking noisily, were looking for food among the overturned earth in the adjoining fields.

She had arrived at last, had reached Ste-Madeleine-de-Beauchamps after a journey which seemed to have lasted interminably!

Marie had warned her not to ask questions at the station.

"They will be curious about you," she said. "Walk straight on down the road towards the sea for about a mile and then turn left."

"For about a mile!" It seemed to Fleur now an insupportable distance.

She looked at the white, dusty road along which several passengers who had disembarked at the same time as herself were already receding.

"If only I could sleep," she thought.

She had spent part of the previous night sitting on a hard bench at a railway terminus. The waiting-room had been closed and locked—German orders, she supposed. Several times during the night officials had

39

walked round, staring disdainfully at the waiting groups of chilled but patient travellers.

The innumerable times that she had shown her papers! Always the same questions, the same explanations.

Once or twice her heart had beat quickly and she had been afraid when she had thought that some inquisitor was staring at her too closely. But the drunken officer who had signed the permits for Monsieur le Maire had been of high standing.

Each time, after some disparaging remarks as to the impropriety of travelling long distances at such a time, her papers were returned and she would take them thankfully conscious that yet another obstacle was passed, another barrier negotiated.

Now, at last, incredibly, she had attained her goal, but was too tired to feel anything save an utter exhaustion. The road stretched ahead. Well, there was nothing for it—she had to go forward.

She walked on, dragging her feet, her luggage impeding her progress as if it contained lumps of lead rather than clothes.

It was hot and she could feel the sweat gathering beneath the stiff band of her hat and trickling down her forehead.

Perhaps it will move some of the dirt, she thought indifferently, knowing how travel-stained and begrimed she was. The carriages in which she had travelled had been filthy, the floors covered not only with dust and dirt, but with pieces of decaying food, paper and ash.

She walked on. Now she could smell and feel the tang of the salt in the air. There was a fresh, invigorating breeze blowing inland from the sea and quite suddenly she was overwhelmed with a longing for England—for home.

On ... on ... the dust rose with every step she took. On ... on ... would the road never come to an end?

More than once she stopped, putting down her luggage, half-tempted to leave it behind and go on without it, trusting to find it again. She would have done so but for the fear that someone might open it and be surprised at the contents.

The road twisted, the fields on both sides were deserted. Fleur saw that now she was walking away from the village. She wondered how much further she must drag herself before she reached the farm.

"You can't miss it," Marie had said, and yet she began to wonder if she had got her instructions right, if she was indeed going in the right direction.

Then, quite suddenly, it lay before her. A turn of the road, the rounding of a great clump of poplar trees, and there it was, a small, untidy building, its walls, once white, now cracked and weather-beaten, a gate swinging back from a broken hinge, a yard deserted save for a tortoise-shell cat sleeping on a wooden bench.

Fleur put down her luggage and stood looking at the house. Only the cat reassured her that someone was at home. She was half-afraid from the general air of desolation and quiet that the place was uninhabited.

Resolutely she picked up her luggage again, rehearsing to herself the words she would say. She crossed the yard and abruptly, deep within the house she heard a dog bark, a sharp, insistent bark as if of fear.

She was conscious then that she was being watched; someone looked through a window swiftly, furtively, and was gone again. There was the sound of a voice, too far off to be intelligible, nevertheless a voice calling, and once again silence.

Fleur reached the porch, she waited a moment, then half-fearfully rapped on the door. She could hardly hear the sound she made herself and she rapped again, this time louder. She waited . . . listening.

After what seemed a long time she heard footsteps. They came nearer the door . . . paused. Someone whispered—she was certain it was a woman—there was the sound of a lock being turned, a bar being lifted.

The door was opened and a man stood there. Fleur

looked at him and knew at once that this was Jacques, Marie's brother. They were very alike; he had the same shaped face, the same eyes of Norman blue, and the same square, sturdy figure.

He was not a young man, his face was deeply scarred with lines and he had too the quiet, sad expression which is often characteristic of those who live near to the soil and learn to accept with a fatalistic melancholy the vagaries of nature.

"What do you want?" Jacques Bouvais spoke slowly, his voice deep and gruff, and to Fleur there was something unfriendly in his attitude.

"I have come to you from your sister Marie."

She looked at him as she spoke the words, expecting an instantaneous response and change of expression. But if he was surprised there was no sign of it on his countenance, only the same look of patient resignation and the same impression of unyielding antagonism.

"Well?" It was a question.

Fleur felt frustrated.

"May I come in?" she asked. "There is so much to explain."

She felt suddenly afraid. Supposing Marie had been wrong, supposing her brother was also one of the collaborators with the German conquerors? In that case she was giving herself completely over to the enemy. And yet what could she do? She had come so far.

"I think you had better explain your business first," Jacques Bouvais replied and suddenly Fleur felt she could bear no more.

She was so tired—too tired to argue, to explain. She was also afraid . . . The glare of the sun had made her eyes ache, she felt now as if she could not trust them to read correctly whether it was friendship or enmity she saw in the face of the man opposite her.

She had put down her wicker basket when she had first come to the door. In her other hand she still held the carpet bag and now it felt as if it was weighing her down, dragging her lower and lower, and she could not

42

resist it. She let it fall and felt the whole earth rocking beneath her, a darkness before her eyes . . .

"I'm all right," she heard herself say, as if she reassured someone else, "if I could only sit down."

Even as she said the words she clutched at her receding senses.

"I have spoken in French," she thought. "I must remember to keep speaking French."

She felt someone's arm round her shoulders, hands were supporting her, and then the glare was gone and she was sitting on a chair in the cool dimness of the house.

"Drink this," a woman's voice said.

There was a glass between her lips and drops of cool, almost icy cold water going slowly down her throat. Her vision cleared, the dizziness went and with it much of her weakness.

"I am sorry," she murmured, "it must have been the heat."

"You have come from Marie?" a soft voice asked, and she looked up to see the gentle face of an elderly woman.

There was no mistaking the kindness of the expression, the tenderness of work-worn hands which still held her arm firmly as if she might be expected to fall from the chair on to the floor.

"I am sorry," Fleur repeated, "but I'm all right again now. Yes, I have come from Marie. She sent me to you. She said you would help me."

She saw a glance pass between the man standing silent on the other side of the room and the woman beside her. She could not interpret it, could not understand what it meant.

"Shall I tell them the truth?" Fleur asked herself. "Dare I?"

And because there seemed no alternative, she looked from one to the other desperately and said in a voice which held a note of despair—

43

"Marie said I could trust you. She told me I would be safe here."

"How do we know that you speak the truth?" the man said suddenly, his voice surly.

Fleur stared at him.

"She did not give me a letter," she replied, "because she told me that you—if you are her brother Jacques—could not read. She told me she had heard that your son had been killed, the priest had written and told her. She described to me how to get here and . . .

Fleur paused a moment and then went on bravely,

". . . she had my papers made out in your name. I was to come to you as your niece, Jeanne Bouvais. Here they are."

She fumbled in her pocket and pulled out the papers which had been handled so often in the last two days. She bent forward and put them on the table. They looked very crumpled and rather dirty, the edges curling round the blue stamp which had made her whole journey possible.

"I have money," Fleur went on. "Marie gave it to me. I can pay for staying here if you will keep me."

It was the woman who spoke quickly.

"She's all right, father, she has come from Marie. Of course she has. How else would she have known about François and that the Padre had written for us. Marie sent you." She turned and peered into Fleur's face. "You swear that? You wouldn't deceive us?"

"But of course not," Fleur replied quickly. "I need your help. Listen, I will conceal nothing, I will tell you the truth. I am English."

The woman beside her gave a start and then she looked across the room at her husband.

"English!" she exclaimed, and then quickly, her voice hardly above a whisper—"Shut the door, father."

The man moved slowly. He locked the door, put back the bolt which Fleur had heard removed. When it was due he came back again and stood, as he had done before, immobile, uncompromising.

44

"But why are you here? Why have you come to us?" the woman asked.

Fleur told them; told them how she had come out to France a few days before the outbreak of war to marry Lucien de Sardou; she told how he had been killed; how she had stayed on, happy at first to be with his mother and then trapped and unable to leave after the German occupation.

She spoke of Marie's kindness to her all through the months when they had lived together, three women isolated in the Château, knowing very little of what was happening in the world outside. Then the Comtesse's death, Monsieur Pierre's arrival and her own flight.

"And what do you want now?" the man asked.

Fleur knew even as he spoke that his antagonism had gone. His voice was impersonal, but the roughness was missing.

"I want to go to England. I want to go home."

She was half-surprised at her own answer. It was the first time she had formulated the idea to herself, but she knew now that the blue of the sea had called her more insistently than she had been aware.

Such a very few miles between her and freedom— surely such an idea was not impossible or impracticable?

"We shall see."

The man turned away and without further words left the room. She could hear his footsteps echoing away into the distance. Fleur turned towards the woman questioningly.

"It is all right," she said reassuringly.

"You mean I can stay?"

"But of course. Marie sent you. Come—bring your things. I will show you to your room."

She picked up the carpet bag and Fleur, carrying the wicker basket, followed her up some twisting, carpetless stairs to the next floor.

The room into which she was shown was low, the rafters quaintly shaped over a small diamond-paned

45

window. There was a huge wooden bedstead taking up half the room and a rough wash-stand on which there was an earthenware bowl and pitcher.

The place was spotlessly clean and there was the faint, sweet smell of hay and of some fragrant herb to which Fleur could not put a name. She glanced out of the window and then exclaimed. She was looking out at the back of the house and to her surprise she found it was far larger than she had at first anticipated.

The door by which she had approached had shown only one small side of the building; behind there were two big wings enclosing a courtyard and from the window Fleur could see many signs of activity.

There were chickens scratching and turning over the trampled-down straw; there was a dog, being dragged along by a small boy who had also a puppy on a string; there were sheds at the far end of the yard and in them Fleur could see the cows standing while they were being milked.

"I had no idea your house was so big!"

"From the front it looks small," Madame Bouvais agreed. "Perhaps it is a good thing. People don't find their way so easily round to the back—it gives us time if strangers come."

Fleur understood, and she noticed on a gate not far from where the cows were being milked an older child was perched, peering this way and that as if keeping sentinel, ready to warn those who were working if anyone should approach unexpectedly.

"It is kind of you to have me," Fleur said impulsively. "I understand just how much I am asking you. I know what it means if we are caught."

Madame Bouvais nodded.

"We have to think of that, we have our family to consider, but my husband is a patriot. He loves France. It breaks his heart to see those *sales Boches* and know that they would strip and starve us to feed their own."

"It is wrong to ask this of you," Fleur said, "but Marie was so certain you would have me. I feel

46

ashamed. I ought really to go away, to take my chance of finding escape through other methods."

"It is not easy," Madame Bouvais replied. "Only last week someone in the village was found sheltering a wounded airman. They were shot—they and their family and one of their friends who had also known that they had him concealed."

Fleur shuddered.

"I have no right to ask it of you," she said again.

"You must be careful, that is all. You are clever, Mademoiselle, and at the moment you would deceive many people."

Fleur glanced in a small mirror hanging on the wall and laughed.

"I look terrible," she exclaimed. "But it is thanks to this dress that I'm here, so I must be grateful. Marie lent it to me."

Madame Bouvais came nearer and touched it.

"I thought I recognised it," she said. "It was Marie's best. She bought it when she was betrothed."

"What happened?" Fleur asked. "She told me it was for her trousseau, but never said why she had not married the man."

"She never told you?" Marie's sister-in-law repeated inquiringly. "Poor soul! Perhaps she is shy to speak of it. She was engaged for a long time—oh, many years, before I married Jacques and came here to live.

"Marie is his eldest sister, but her sisters married before her although she was the first to be betrothed. The young man's father was an old friend of the family. That Marie should espouse his son was arranged almost while they were still children.

"But there were difficulties. Marie's fiancé was a fisherman; the seasons were bad; year after year the wedding was postponed. Marie's *dot* was complete, her trousseau was ready, but the young man could not complete his side of the bargain.

"Then at last everything was settled and the date fixed. Marie was excited; she had been afraid if she waited much longer she would '*coiffer* Ste Catherine.' But Grandpère, Marie's father, was a gambler—he loved to take a chance, you understand. He would gamble on many things, on which boat would bring in the largest catch, on whose bitch would pup first, on whose farm-cart could carry the greatest load the longest distance.

"He was many things in his time—fisherman, farmer, mayor of Ste-Madeleine; but always, always, he was a gambler and nothing could stop him. He had been well off, for he had inherited a great deal of land; but he gambled a good part of it away. Only this farm remained and that too I believe would have gone if he had not died."

"And Marie?" Fleur asked, sensing the inevitable end of the story.

"Marie's *dot* went—one evening in June. It was on a race, a race of boats as to who could round the buoy the quickest. The old man was so certain that he had chosen the right one.

"There was an advocate, nearly as bad as he was himself, living in the place then. He was a greedy man and he would always take bet in cash rather than in kind. He incited Grandpère, taunted him and jeered at him until the old man came back here and, taking Marie's *dot* from its hiding-place beneath his bed, carried it down to the quay. No one realised what he was doing until it was too late—the money was wagered and lost."

"And because of that Marie's fiancé would not marry her?" Fleur cried in horror. "How despicable, how mean!"

"But how could he without her *dot*? He had depended on it, you see; the sum had been arranged. And there was another girl who had always wanted him. She was wealthy and her parents were anxious for the match.

"They were married within three months, and Marie went away to service to the Comtesse. She was lucky to get such a position—we have often envied her."

48

"Envied her!" Fleur exclaimed. "When she might have been married with a home of her own. How could you?"

"It was a privilege to serve anyone so gracious as the Comtesse. Often she would send us little messages. Once, when my children were ill, we received a present of money and fruit from the estate. We were very proud of the connection. Marie did well for herself."

Fleur knew there was nothing she could say, but she felt as if the dress that she wore was the expression of a tragedy beyond words, a tragedy of a life broken and ruined through greed—the greed of money.

"And now, Mademoiselle . . ."

Fleur interrupted Madame Bouvais.

"Isn't it unwise to call me Mademoiselle?" she asked. "Perhaps while I am here I had better be Jeanne."

"It seems wrong somehow, too familiar . . ."

"Not really," Fleur replied. "Not when you think of what you are doing for me."

Madame Bouvais smiled and her smile was curiously sweet.

"We are glad to do it," she said quietly, "even though you must forgive me if it makes me—sometimes—a little afraid."

CHAPTER FIVE

Supper was over—a scanty meal composed mostly of vegetables and potatoes, augmented with a somewhat watery soup from the stockpot.

The children wiped their plates with pieces of coarse bread, stuffing it into their mouths and looking wistfully towards the empty dishes as if they half-hoped by some miracle they would be filled again.

"*C'est fini, mes enfants,*" Madame Bouvais said with a firmness which brooked no argument, and there was an audible sigh from several small throats. Their father said grace and a babble of voices broke out, as laughing and teasing each other they ran into the yard.

Fleur rose to help Madame Bouvais clear the dishes. She carried them into a small scullery and piled them in the sink.

When she returned to the kitchen, she was surprised to see her hostess pull from the oven a bowl of soup and a dish on which was piled a big helping of vegetables.

'Is there someone coming in late?' Fleur wondered.

There had been no empty place at the table which had seemed overcrowded with a surprising number of children. The only outsider besides herself was a farm hand, an uncouth youth with a withered arm who had been left in Jacques Bouvais's employment because he was no use in any other capacity.

Suzanne, the oldest daughter, an attractive girl of seventeen, came back through the kitchen door.

"Shall I take it down to him, *Maman*?" she asked; then saw Fleur standing there in the door of the scullery. She bit her lips and glanced at her mother as if embarrassed.

Madame Bouvais hesitated; then, as if making up her mind, she placed the things on a tray and turning to Fleur said—

"Go with Suzanne. There is something you had better learn. Also it should please you."

Fleur looked at her in surprise. Suzanne, picking up the tray, asked shyly:

"Won't you come with me, Mademoiselle?"

"Of course," Fleur replied; then questioned: "Is there another member of the family? There are a great many of you."

The girl smiled mischievously and there were dimples at the corners of her mouth.

"Yes, one of the family, Mademoiselle. Come and see him."

She turned towards the door which stood at the far end of the kitchen and opened it to reveal a flight of stone steps going down into the darkness of what appeared to be a cellar. She started to descend.

Fleur wonderingly followed her. The cool air was pleasant after the hot, steamy atmosphere of the kitchen. They descended quite a long way; the cellar was deep, well below ground Fleur imagined. They crossed a flagged floor between stacks of old barrels, boxes and crates.

A thin light came through a grating high against the roof and it was possible, as soon as her eyes became accustomed to the dimness, to see that the cellar extended some way.

Suzanne walked to the far end. Here, so far as Fleur could see, was a blank wall, with an empty crate lying propped against it. Suzanne put the tray into Fleur's hands, moved the box, and then, putting her finger to

51

her lips, she knocked on the wall three times. After a moment's pause, there came an answering knock—one, two, three.

Suzanne raised her hand above her head to press some secret catch hidden beneath the heavy beam, a panel in the wall slid back and there was an opening.

Fleur stood watching in astonishment, too surprised to move until Suzanne, taking the tray from her, said in a low voice:

"*Venez,* Mademoiselle, follow me."

They passed through the opening. They were in another cellar, much smaller than the first, but here the light was stronger. There were two ventilators and one of them had been hinged open so that a small square opening let in both light and air. In the centre of the room arranged on a square of rush matting stood a table and a chair and in the corner a low bed.

Fleur stared, for sitting on the bed was a man, a young man, who said in French as they entered:

"Welcome, *ma petite* Suzanne, I have been waiting for you. I'm so hungry I could eat a whole ox."

"I'm afraid I can't bring you that," Suzanne replied giggling, "but I bring you something more interesting, Monsieur—a friend."

The man got slowly and with difficulty to his feet. Fleur saw that his foot was swathed in bandages, then as he rose she gave an exclamation for he was wearing the blue uniform of the R.A.F.

"You are English!" The words burst from her and he stared at her in surprise.

"Yes, I am," he answered in the same language, "but . . ."

He looked at Fleur's dress, the dark voluminous skirts, the high-necked, tightly buttoned bodice, at her hair scraped into a bun at the nape of the neck.

"Yes, English," he said, and self-consciously raised her hands to the nakedness of her ears and temples.

"Are you really? My goodness! That's marvellous!"

There was something eager and boyish in his excitement. Fleur found herself moving forward automatically, holding out both her hands.

"You are wounded. How did you get here?"

"I baled out," he said, smiling as if it was the greatest joke in the world. "And if it hadn't been for those good people I should either be dead or in a prison camp. They brought me here when I was still unconscious and have hidden me ever since. But you—what are you doing here?"

"I am hiding too. At least, they are hiding me. But oh! How amazingly good it is of them to take the risk a second time."

She understood now the Bouvais's suspicion at her appearance, their reluctance to let her in, the glances that had passed between man and wife when she had first arrived.

She found to her embarrassment that she was still holding the unknown airman's hands—both of them—in her own.

She had an uncomfortable suspicion that in another moment she might have put her arms round him and kissed him—it was so wonderful to find a fellow-countryman here in France. There was something too exhilarating in it for conventionality.

She moved away from him and glanced at Suzanne who was standing regarding them with an expression of delight on her face.

"You are happy?" she asked, including them both in her question.

"Very," the airman replied in French. "You are a magician—you not only save my life with your good food, you bring me a companion as well. Suzanne, I salute you!"

The girl giggled, then asked:

"Mademoiselle will stay a little while? I will come back later. It is wise to lock the door."

"But of course," the airman replied. "We must be doubly careful now we have Mademoiselle to guard as well."

Suzanne smiled and departed; the panel in the wall swung back into position, there was a little click and they heard her replace the crate as it had been before and move away, her footsteps quiet, but distinct on the stone flags.

Fleur felt a sudden shyness creep over her now that they were alone, but the airman was quite at his ease. He hobbled to the table, drawing up the chair.

"Do you mind if I eat? I'm ravenous."

"But, of course."

He looked at the food, picked up a spoon, then inquired: "You won't share it? You've had some, I mean?"

"Yes, I have already had my supper."

He waited for no further reassurance, but started to eat hungrily and in great mouthfuls.

"Talk to me," he said. "Tell me about yourself. Why are you here? What is your name?"

"I have had so many names," Fleur replied. "At the moment my papers are made in that of Jeanne Bouvais. I am supposed to be Suzanne's cousin."

"But in reality you are . . ."

"Fleur Garton."

She did not know why, but she found it hard to say her surname; it was so long it had passed her lips, and how commonplace it sounded after de Malmont and de Sardou.

"Garton. I seem to know the name."

"And yours?"

"Jack Reynolds."

"How long have you been here?"

"Let me see—it must be nearly two months by now. I was pretty bad when they first picked me up. Had to bale out—machine was shot to pieces. My tail gunner was dead, anyway."

"Wasn't it fearfully dangerous? I mean for the Bouvais."

"They must have been crazy to run such a risk. The Germans were looking for me, I believe. Luckily I had baled out at a pretty good height—they had a fairly wide area to search. The Bouvais family have been goodness itself, and yet sometimes I wonder what will be the end of it."

"Have you any plans for escape?"

"None, unless I can persuade them to risk taking me across the Channel."

"That's what I want."

"By Jove! It would be marvellous if we could get away together. I've made a lot of plans, of course—I haven't got much else to think about. Now we can make them together. The point is—I haven't got any money. I hate to ask so much and give nothing in exchange."

"I have got plenty."

"You're lucky! But tell me about yourself. Why are you here at all?"

Fleur told her story simply. She ended it about the same time as her listener finished his meal.

He wiped the plate with a piece of bread just as the children had done and sat back with the same wistful sigh of dissatisfaction. He looked up, caught Fleur's watchful eye and laughed.

"Don't look so surprised. I'm still hungry and not ashamed to admit it. Do you remember how we used to be told that it was good for us to get up from the table unsatisfied? Well, I must be qualifying for some very special sort of Heaven at the moment."

Then, before Fleur could speak, he added quickly: "I'm not being rude. I've been listening to every word you said. It's an exciting story—rather like an unfinished serial in a magazine. By Jove! When you come to think of it, you and I might be the heroine and hero of a best-seller."

"As long as it has a happy ending," Fleur retorted.

"Must have. If only this damned foot of mine would get all right, I could get out at night and scout round a bit—get to know the country and watch for a chance to escape. At the moment I daren't move, I have to remain here. I mustn't even go upstairs except on special occa-

55

sions and at night. It takes me too long to get down again, you see."

"Do the Germans come here often?"

"They have been several times since I've been here. Once they searched the cellar—I heard them poking about among the crates. That was a bad moment, I can tell you; but somehow, they never suspected a second cellar."

"Did the Bouvais build it specially for you?" Fleur asked curiously.

"Heavens, no! It's always been there. I imagine it was intended for a hidey-hole from the start. This isn't the first time the cellar has been used to hide fugitives or illicit goods."

"I still can't get over finding you," Fleur said impulsively. "It's the last thing I expected, somehow."

"But you're pleased?" he asked, and she smiled her reply frankly and without pretence.

It was at that moment they heard footsteps coming across the outer cellar.

"That must be Suzanne," Fleur said, but Jack Reynolds hushed her into silence. They both stood motionless until Suzanne's knock came on the wall.

"Never take chances," the airman said reprovingly. "We expected Suzanne, but if it had been anyone else they might have heard your voice."

"I'm sorry," Fleur apologised.

"We haven't got only ourselves to think of," he continued; "we have them too. If we are found here, they will be put up against a wall, every man jack of them."

"Yes, I realise that," Fleur said humbly.

He gave the answering signal and the panel slipped back.

"*Vous avez fini?*" Suzanne asked. She picked up the tray, but her words included more than the eating of the meal.

"I had better go," Fleur said quickly. "Good night . . ." She hesitated and looked at the blue line on his sleeve. "Is it Mr.?"

"Pilot officer," he replied, "if you want to be correct. But I'd rather you said Jack—it sounds more homely."

"Good night then, Jack."

"Good night, Fleur."

He took her hand for a moment. She felt there was so much more she wanted to ask him, so much left unsaid, but instead she turned away and followed Suzanne.

The panel slipped back into place, she helped the girl move the crate and then they were walking across the cellar in silence, Fleur purposely making her footsteps as light as possible until they reached the stairs leading up to the kitchen.

Madame Bouvais was washing up.

"It was a surprise, yes?"

"A tremendous surprise," Fleur answered. "Oh, Madame, how good you and your husband are! I feel ashamed to ask you to take further risks."

Madame Bouvais smiled.

"Now don't worry your head," she said. "Everything will come right in time. We must be patient."

Fleur picked up a cloth and started to dry the plates which had been washed.

"Let Suzanne do that," Madame suggested, but Fleur shook her head.

"While I am here I must behave like a dutiful niece."

The two women worked for a few moments in silence, then Fleur asked—"What about clothes, Madame? Would it be indiscreet, dangerous, to wear some of my own things?"

Madame Bouvais looked worried.

"They are good?" she asked. "Perhaps smart?"

"I'm afraid they would appear so, but I can't go on wearing this dress always—or do you think it would be safer?"

"Suzanne has a dress. It is her best, she had been saving it, but she will be glad to give it to you. When you are working you can put an apron over it."

"But I can't take Suzanne's best dress!" Fleur expostulated.

"Suzanne will be glad to make a sacrifice too," her mother said firmly.

Later, when Fleur was going to bed, there came a knock at her door. Suzanne came into the room carrying in her arms a dress of pink and white cotton. It was simply made with a square neck, a tight waist and a full skirt; but it was fresh and clean and Suzanne carried it almost reverently, as if it was something infinitely precious.

Fleur glanced at her face and knew at once how much it meant to the girl to part with this frock, her only decent one, the one in which, perhaps, she hoped to fascinate some stalwart young fisherman.

Fleur pulled her wicker basket out from a corner where it had lain since her arrival and unstrapping it began to pull out the frocks Marie had placed there so carefully.

There were several of them—a black crêpe-de-chine afternoon dress, a frock of royal blue crêpe, a white linen with a red coat trimmed with glass buttons, a green voile with lace trimmings. Fleur laid them on the bed as Suzanne stood watching her wide-eyed. When the box was empty Fleur turned with a gesture.

"Look," she said. "You are kind enough to give me your dress—I will give you one of mine. Perhaps it won't be wise for you to wear it at once, not until either I have gone away or the war is ended, but you must take your choice. Have which you like—it is a fair exchange."

Suzanne's eyes shone. For a moment she expostulated . . . made polite protestations . . . she was only too glad to do something for Mademoiselle . . . she wanted nothing in return. Fleur laughed at her.

"I insist, Suzanne! Whichever one you want is yours."

Suzanne touched the dresses tentatively as if she was afraid the roughness of her fingers would harm them.

Finally, after a long time, when she had held each one against her glowing face and seen it reflected in the small mirror, she decided on the royal blue crêpe. It was a little old for her, Fleur thought, but nevertheless she could understand that the richness of the material and the colour might be more alluring than any of the others.

"Never, Mademoiselle," Suzanne said passionately, "never, never have I had anything so beautiful. I shall treasure it always."

Fleur could somehow believe that, seeing that Marie had kept the dress she wore for nearly thirty years.

I only hope, she thought to herself, that she will have the sense to wear it while she is still young and attractive. It won't do her much good if she becomes an old maid.

Clasping her dress tightly to her breast, still incoherent with thanks, Suzanne slipped from the room.

Fleur repacked the dresses and put them away in the wicker basket. It was not safe to leave them lying about.

Then she undressed, taking off Marie's dress with a thankfulness which was almost ingratitude. It had served its purpose, it had stood her in good stead, yet somehow she hated the dark thick sombreness of it.

She looked in the carpet bag for a nightgown, found one and slipped it over her head. She released her hair and brushed it, noting how it fell softly into its accustomed waves on either side of her forehead.

The prim peasant girl was gone, it was a familiar face, attractive and appealing, which looked back at her out of the small mirror.

Let's hope no Germans come searching the house tonight, she thought, or they'll get a shock.

Pulling the curtains across the open window, she crept across the room and into the big square bed.

"I've got here," Fleur thought triumphantly as she closed her eyes, ready to drift into that deep restful sleep for which her tired body had been aching. "I've got here, and now the next step is to cross the Channel, to find my way home to England . . ."

CHAPTER SIX

"I've got news for you, Jack."

Fleur threw herself down on the soft straw. She was panting a little, her face in the light of a full moon eager and excited.

"What is it?" Jack Reynolds asked turning quickly towards her. "I wondered why you were late."

"Just as I was coming out Henri arrived back from the village. There's a chance—a very good chance— that he will be able to buy a boat in a few weeks' time!"

"A motor boat?"

"Yes, it has a motor. It is a ketch, a large one, which the owner has been using for fishing but finds too expensive to run. Henri says he is talking of selling it and he won't hesitate once he knows he can get his price in gold."

"I say, Fleur, how marvellous!" Jack sat forward eagerly, his hands clasped round his knees.

For over a fortnight now it had been their habit—his and Fleur's—to meet outside after the family had gone to bed. It was the only time that Jack dared leave his cellar to get some fresh air and exercise, and gradually Fleur had got into the habit of joining him.

Jack's leg was much better, but it was not only his lameness which made it dangerous to go far; for that matter they hardly dared to leave the shadow of the farm.

They would walk up and down then, if the evening was warm, or sit and talk, finding it harder every passing hour to say good night.

Fleur hardly dared admit to herself how much she looked forward to these meetings. The daytime passed slowly, the hours seemed to drag by while she would help in the house, assist on the farm, or do any of the hundred and one little jobs which always seemed to be waiting for a pair of idle hands.

The ordinary routine of farmwork was considerably augmented by the continual fear of inquisitive strangers, of Germans who might come for an inspection of the stock and might by some mischance find other things as well.

There was so much to hide. Jack and herself, Fleur discovered, were not the only things that the Bouvais kept concealed; there were many other reasons why one of the children should act sentinel on the farm gate.

All the livestock on the place were supposed to be accounted for to the Germans, while in fact only a very small proportion were. At the first sign of anybody approaching, the sound of a car turning into the lane or the appearance of an unknown figure in the distance, someone would give the alarm.

Instantly most of the hens, the pigs, and even one of the cows were spirited away into special hiding-places.

Fleur often wondered how the Bouvais dared defy the regulations. The penalties for the slightest infringement were brutal but she came to realise that the Germans, try as they might, could not destroy that unquenchable defiance, it was the true spirit of freedom which would never be stamped out save by death.

More than once Fleur thought how much Jacques Bouvais had in common with her own countrymen. The Norman strain was in both. William the Conqueror was responsible for many characteristics on both sides of the Channel.

Soon after Fleur's arrival Jacques had begun to talk quite seriously of how she and Jack could get to En-

61

gland. She soon realised that he enjoyed making plans; coming back from his day's work always ready with some new suggestion, some new idea which they would discuss solemnly and critically, most of them to be discarded as too risky.

Then, unexpectedly, Henri, who was nearly eighteen and the eldest of the family since his brother's death, announced that he too intended to go to England.

"I must join the Free French," he said. "I want to fight for France."

His pronouncement was made late one evening when the children had gone to bed and only his father and mother, Fleur and Jack were in the kitchen.

For a moment there was silence; then Fleur saw the slow, painful tears gather in Madame Bouvais's tired eyes, in her lap her hands clenched and unclenched themselves convulsively. Without a word she rose from the table and went to the window. Her back was turned to the others, but they knew that she was striving for self-control.

It was Jacques who spoke first.

"Your brother died for France." His voice was grave.

"I am prepared to die too, if need be," young Henri replied, his voice raised a little with the emotion of the moment "It is better than a living death, at any rate. What else does existence here under these devils offer us?"

There was silence again and everyone was conscious of Madame Bouvais. They waited for her. She turned round suddenly and walked across the room to her son.

"It is right that you should go," she said and, bending, kissed him on the forehead.

"I'm sorry, Mother," the boy said.

"You are not to be sorry," she replied. "We have given François to our country already, we hoped to be spared further sacrifice, but you are right, *mon fils*—it is no life for you here. Go to England, join the brave General de Gaulle—he is our only hope. When he returns with the British Army, the German plunderers will be driven back at the point of the bayonet."

It was bravely spoken. Fleur felt they ought to applaud her; instead they sat silent and embarrassed, while the tears ran unchecked down Madame Bouvais's face.

"But the point is how to get to England?" Jack said, and his words broke the emotional tension.

"That, indeed, is the point," Jacques Bouvais responded.

They had long ago decided that it was impossible to set forth in the only boat which belonged to the Bouvais family. It had no engine and required three strong men at least to row it any distance.

"You would be picked up by the patrol," Henri told them. "The only chance, and it is a slender one, is to go out with the fishing fleet and then make a dash for it."

Fleur had suggested taking some of the other fishermen into their confidence, but Jacques was against it.

"Our neighbours have all suffered already," he said, "and the last reprisals against the family who housed the wounded airman have made them afraid. Also there is a high price on the head of every Englishman who is turned over to the authorities.

"Many people down in the village are hungry. It is hard to turn one's children empty from the table when a fortune is there for the taking. No, it is unwise to share one's secret—let us keep it to ourselves. We will find a way."

Fleur, listening to Henri tonight, believed that their patient waiting had at last been rewarded—a boat such as he described would indeed give them that slender chance of escape.

"What worries me," Jack said, "is how we are going to get to the beach."

"Henri has thought of that," Fleur replied. "He is going to bring the ketch round to the creek in the cliffs—that is the nearest point to the house. There he will be overlooked by the coastguards, but the guards are new, a fresh face will mean nothing to them. You can go disguised as a fisherman and once in the boat must lie concealed while Henri takes her round to the quay. He has other ideas of how to get me aboard."

"What sort of ideas?"

"Well, I think the most feasible is to wrap me in the fishing nets and carry me over his shoulder. I warned him I was no lightweight, but Henri is a strong young man and I don't think that will worry him."

"But who is going out with us in the boat?" Jack asked. "Henri's not going to pretend that he is going out fishing single-handed?"

"No, Jacques is coming," Fleur replied, "and when we get some way out to sea he is going to say that he feels ill. He can then be transferred to the boat which has got the largest catch and will therefore be going back first. Henri is to linger until the last, saying he has been unfortunate, and then when most of the fleet have turned for home, he will make a dash for it."

"Let's hope the motor is powerful and the visibility bad!"

"Like Madame Bouvais, we can only hope and pray."

"She has been good about it, hasn't she?"

Fleur nodded.

"She adores Henri, too, it is easy to see that. I think he is the favourite of her children."

"I wonder how we should behave in like circumstances," Jack Reynolds said reflectively. "I wonder if many people in England would shelter a Frenchman, and a Frenchwoman they had never seen before, knowing that they risked not only their own lives, but those of their children as well?"

"I like to think I should be so noble," Fleur answered, "and yet sometimes I am afraid that I should fail both the refugees and my own ideals."

"I'm quite certain you wouldn't do that," Jack retorted with an accent on the pronoun.

"Why?" Fleur asked curiously.

"I don't believe you'd fail anyone."

She smiled at him lightly.

"Thank you for the compliment."

"Actually it wasn't meant to be one. I was only speaking of something of which I am absolutely certain."

"Thank you again," she murmured, but she realised that her lightness was out of place. He was speaking seriously, intensely; quite suddenly he put out his hand and put it over hers.

"I wonder if you realise, Fleur, how much it has meant to me having you here. When you came, I was almost at breaking-point. I was feeling I couldn't stand it any longer, being cooped up with nothing to do, nobody to talk to, and then suddenly you appeared. It gave me new life just to look at you, to hear your voice, and then—well, you know what happened then."

"What?" Fleur had to ask the question; she felt as if the word forced itself between her lips.

"I fell in love with you, of course."

She wanted to laugh lightly and happily, but somehow she could not. Instead she dropped her eyes, feeling a warm happiness creep over her.

"Fleur, tell me you love me. I want you so damnably. I can't bear it if you don't care."

It was a cry of desperation, a cry such as a child, frightened and perturbed, might have made. Instinctively Fleur responded to it.

"I think I do, Jack."

"Say it," he insisted, "say the words."

She was shy and her voice was hardly above a whisper.

"I . . . I love you!"

He gave a little cry and then buried his head against her breast. She clasped her arms round him and held him thus, securely, comfortingly.

"I love you so," he reiterated. "I can't live without you, Fleur, I can think of nothing else. I go to sleep at night dreaming of you; I wake in the morning longing for you and counting the hours and minutes until I see you.

Suddenly his arms were round her, his lips were on hers, fierce and hungry, demanding, beseeching.

"Jack, please!"

She tried to free herself, tried to hold him off for a moment while she could think, while the chaotic inconsequence of her thoughts could steady itself, but it was no use.

"Fleur! . . . Fleur! . . ." Over and over again he repeated her name, straining her closer and closer to him.

"Darling, please . . . please . . ."

Her cry reached him. He let her go, taking his arms away so that her head fell back against the rick. She could see his expression in the moonlight. Fleur was breathing quickly, one hand quieting the tumult within her breast where his head had lain.

The country lay white and still before them, the shadows of the tall poplar trees were heavy, purple and mysterious.

It was a night of beauty, a night of such loveliness that it seemed to hold a magic indescribable in words; and they were isolated; two people alone together in a world of their own.

The past had slipped away . . . had gone . . . the future was problematical. There was just the present, pulsating, wonderful—and yet, in some way all its own, frightening.

"I love . . . you, Jack," Fleur repeated the words again as if to reassure herself rather than him.

"I worship you, Fleur. Be kind to me."

She felt a sudden surging tenderness. She reached out her hand and touched his cheek; it was warm beneath her fingers, slightly rough.

"I do really love you, Jack," she repeated gently.

"You do?" He asked the question eagerly. "Then . . . oh, Fleur . . . if you love me . . . ?"

He swept her into his arms, kissing her wildly, frantically, as if she gave him a new life and a new hope.

"Love me, Fleur . . . love me," he pleaded. "Want you . . . I must have you!"

Fleur was suddenly still. She liked him, she wanted to make him happy . . . to help and comfort him. Then she remembered Sylvia and every instinct in her body revolted. She could not be like that—it was impossible!

"No, Jack," she said gently. "We can't spoil anything so perfect . . . so sacred . . . and so wonderful as our love."

He hid his face against her neck. She knew she had disappointed and perhaps hurt him, but what he asked was impossible.

She must try to make him understand, help him to wait until they were free and married before their love could be absolutely perfect.

But in the meantime they could be very happy.

* * *

It was very late when Fleur and Jack went back to the house. They moved quietly through the yard, Jack's arm round Fleur's shoulders, their steps matched so that they walked in unison.

The door into the kitchen was unlatched, there was the faint smell of food and the sense of being enclosed in the soft, warm darkness. Jack shut the door behind him and reaching out his hands found Fleur again. She nestled close to him.

He sought her lips and then buried his face for a moment against the firmness of her neck.

"You're perfect—you know that. I didn't know a woman could be so sweet."

"Go to bed, darling, you're tired."

He held her very close, kissing her lips, her eyes, her hair, then slowly and reluctantly they separated, Jack moving towards the cellar door. She waited to hear him grope for the catch and put forward his foot, tentatively feeling for the first step down, before she turned away towards the stairs.

"Good night, my darling," she whispered, "good night."

She crept upstairs. The latch of her door creaked, but there were reassuring sounds of heavy breathing coming from the other rooms along the passage.

In her own bedroom Fleur pulled back the window curtains; the light was faint, very faint, but enough for her to see without a candle.

She slipped off her clothes, then resting her arms on the window ledge, her chin on her hands, looked out at the sky from which the stars had faded.

"I am happy," she said aloud. "I am happy and I shall make him happy. Do you understand, Lucien?"

*   *   *

It was midday before Fleur went down to the cellar to see Jack.

"Shall I take the *déjeuner* below?" she asked Madame Bouvais, as the family began to come in from the yard.

"It is ready," Madame replied, pouring out a liberal helping of soup and cutting a large slice from the loaf which had to serve everybody.

Fleur lifted the tray in her hands. She crossed the cellar, went through the usual precautions of knocking, then slid back the panel. She was hardly inside Jack's room before his arms were round her.

"Why haven't you come before?" he asked, kissing her so that his lunch was in imminent danger of being spilled. "I have been worried ... frightened. Why are you so late?"

"Wait a minute, let me put down the tray."

He took it from her and laid it on the table.

"Sure you still love me?"

"Quite sure!"

"I love you so! Oh, Fleur, I love you!"

"I am glad," she whispered, "so terribly glad. And I love you too. I have been thinking of you all the morning, longing for this moment when I could come to you."

"You've driven me nearly mad waiting here, not knowing what you were feeling. I thought that you wouldn't come."

"How stupid you are!" She reached up and put her arms round his neck, drawing his face down to hers.

He held her close, his grasp getting more possessive, his hand slipping from her shoulder to her breast.

"'I must go," she said, "they are waiting for me upstairs."

He released her reluctantly.

"You will come back later?"

"Of course I will."

She raised her lips to his, then slipped away from him, put the panel back into place and, hurrying across the cellar, climbed the stairs to the kitchen.

The family were all sitting round the table as Fleur slipped into her place with what she hoped was an unself-conscious air. She saw Suzanne glance at her and then across at her brother Henri. They exchanged a knowing smile. Henri winked.

Oh, these French! Fleur thought, half-amused, half-irritated. One can keep nothing from them—if it concerns love!

CHAPTER SEVEN

"Do you realise it's our last day, that tomorrow we shall not be here?" Jack asked.

"Don't count your chickens," Fleur admonished, looking round the tiny cell which had housed him for nearly four months. "There's a lot of if's about it. If the weather is fine ... If Henri is quite certain that the motor is going perfectly ... If he can get us down to the boat ... and last, but rather important—if we can get away undetected."

"Don't be so gloomy," Jack retorted; and getting up from the table, he went and stood by the open ventilator. "If it's a day like this, we couldn't ask for anything better."

There was a thin sea-mist outside; the light in the cellar was dim.

"Aren't you excited?" Jack went on. He lit a cigarette and sitting down on his bed, put up his feet.

"I ought to be, oughtn't I?" Fleur replied; "and yet ... I don't know ... it's difficult to put into words, but somehow I'm afraid, not of the danger, but of leaving here, of relinquishing the security I know for an unknown future."

"The security of a prison?"

"I suppose it does seem like that to you! To me—well, it has been very happy."

"Darling!"—Jack sat forward and stretched out his arms to her.

Fleur smiled, but shook her head, and moving away from him, perched herself on the table, her feet on the seat of the only chair.

"Does that seem strange to you?" she asked. "But I have been happy, you know, terribly happy, and I'm afraid that everything may be altered when we get back to England."

"You're being silly," Jack said affectionately. "We shall still go on being happy—you and I—for ever and ever."

"Are you sure?" Fleur asked. "You'll go back to your work—to your Squadron, while I have got to start my life all over again."

"What are you going to do?"

"I honestly don't know. Find out how much money I've got, first of all. I suppose there is some left, if my stepmother hasn't taken it all—and then ..." Fleur hesitated, but bravely she said the words, her eyes seeking his, "it rather depends on you."

"On me?" Jack asked. "Oh, but of course, darling. We'll get married; but we mustn't do anything in too much of a hurry. You must come down to my mother's with me while we talk it all over."

"What will your mother think of me?"

"What could she think except that you are the most wonderful person in the world?"

Somehow, Fleur wasn't convinced. Jack was always reticent where his family was concerned; she couldn't get a clear picture of them from what he had told her and the way he had described them. Now she felt suddenly afraid of this strange woman who had the first claim on Jack.

Every day her love for him had grown. He seemed to twine himself round her heart. She loved the boyish eagerness with which he grasped at their love and made it the axis of their very existence.

71

She loved his impatience with everybody and everything that kept her from him even for a few minutes.

She loved too, although she protested against it, the way he brushed aside all conventionality, making it obvious even to the Bouvais that they were in love.

They played absurd, tender little games together; they laughed almost continuously; words came tumbling to their lips in the exuberance of youth.

Sometimes Fleur wondered if despite all her love for Jack she really understood him, if she in reality knew more than his superficial charms.

Now she felt a sinking within herself, a jealousy which could not be denied, as she realised how greatly Jack was looking forward to tomorrow.

He was nervous, tense and excited. He had walked up and down the cellar a thousand times that morning, going over the plans of escape again and again in case they should have forgotten something—the things they would take with them, the way they would go, the explanation which Henri must be ready to offer should there be any hitch.

Their plans had been changed slightly in the last few days because an acquaintance of Henri's had decided to go with them. He was a young man of good family whose father owned a small estate in the neighbourhood.

Now they would leave with the fishing fleet with ostensibly two men aboard, and it gave them a better chance when they were once out to sea to have three men to look after the sails and attend to the motor.

"We'll have to use everything we've got to get up enough speed to avoid the patrol," Henri had told them.

There was something in the thought of being chased, perhaps of being caught, that made Fleur's heart beat and made her desperately afraid of the project. But Jack, she knew, was merely excited at the whole idea.

He reached out his arms now and held her close.

"Do you love me?"

"I adore you. You know that."

"Stroke my forehead, you know I love the feel of your fingers."

She did as she was told, moving her fingers gently until his eyes closed in lazy contentment.

"It's a funny thing, isn't it?" she said after a few minutes, "that war can bring so much misery and sorrow and yet such happiness as well. If it hadn't been for the war, you see, I should have never met you."

"I certainly shouldn't have been here," Jack replied. "I should have been in the old motor works—my nose to the grindstone. Not that I wasn't just beginning to do pretty well."

"What's happened to them now?"

"The motor works? Oh, they are turning out aeroplanes and have been enlarged to twice their size. I hardly recognise the place when I pass it."

"It's near your home, isn't it?"

"Just round the corner, up the hill and straight on."

"Don't be so ridiculous!"

"Well, it's the truth. About three miles, in actual fact. I used to go over to my motor bicycle—it seemed more distinguished, somehow, than catching the 8.15 in a bowler hat. That was the choice I had to make—an office boy in my father's bank or a workman in greasy overalls in Mitcham's Motor Works. The engines won—I never could resist them."

"I'm sure you were quite outstandingly brilliant," Fleur said teasingly. "And one day you would have owned the works."

Jack laughed.

"Hardly that. If you saw the boss, you'd be quite certain that 'what I have, I hold' is his motto. He's a fine chap all the same, you must have heard of him."

"Who?—Mr. Mitcham?"

"Sir Norman Mitcham, please—he's one of the big Captains of industry, small-town boy makes good and all that sort of thing. He started at the bottom and got to the top a good deal quicker than most people.

"If you saw him, you wouldn't be surprised—he's

like a Juggernaut, crushing everything under him. I'm not certain we didn't all have a bit of hero-worship for him in the works, at the same time—my goodness we'd toe the line if he was anywhere about!"

"And when the war's over, will you go back into Mitcham Motors?"

Jack hesitated a moment.

"I suppose so. Although I'm not certain I wouldn't rather stay in the R.A.F. if there was a chance for me to do that. I love flying—I think I love it more than anything else in the world."

"More than you love me?" Fleur heard herself ask, and was ashamed of the femininity of the remark.

"You can't compare the two," Jack prevaricated.

Then, grinning at the disappointment in her eyes, he drew her face down to his and kissed her.

"I love you, darling, and can't think of anything else at the moment, not even of slipping in and out of the clouds or the thrill of shooting down a Hun. I just want to lie here and purr like a cat while you stroke my forehead."

"I spoil you. It was a mistake from the beginning."

"Was it?"

He sat up and held her close; his lips sought hers again; she felt a sweet languor creep over her and she could not resist the possessive passion of him.

"You're so sweet, my Fleur."

For a moment she let herself drift in a Heaven of close intimacy, then resolutely she pushed him away.

"Let's be sensible," she said, and her voice was deep and moved. "It's nearly supper-time, I must go and help Madame Bouvais get it ready."

"Our last supper here," Jack stretched his arms above his head.

But Fleur knew that it was only a gesture, for his muscles were not relaxed, he was tense and alert, waiting, longing for the morrow.

She went out of the cellar, closing the secret panel, and climbed the steps to the kitchen. Madame Bouvais was bending over the oven, Henri was sitting on one of the wooden stools at the table, his head in his hands. There was something in his attitude which made Fleur exclaim.

"What's the matter? Is something wrong?"

At the sight of her he looked round quickly to see if they were being overheard and then started to pour forth his words, quickly, vehemently.

Fleur listened ... her face slowly whitened. Henri had indeed brought bad news. The Germans had announced that on the morrow there was to be an inspection of fishing-boats; there was the likelihood of some being moved to another area, the owners would have to go with them.

With the turbulent emotionalism of his race, Henri, who had been so confident, so excited through all their planning, was now in the depths of despair. He was sure that his new, and to him, beautiful boat would attract attention; he was certain that both he and it were likely to be sent away.

Fleur heard the note of anguish in his voice and in her mind she heard it echoed by Jack. Although they were of such different races, the two young men were not unlike—both prone to wild enthusiasms and equally wild despairs.

If things went wrong for them personally, it seemed as if the end of the world had come and that there was no hope, no possible chance of resuscitation in the future.

Fleur stood still, her fingers linked together tightly. What could she do, she thought; she couldn't bear that Jack should be disappointed. She knew that she would be the one to tell him.

It was as if she must deprive a dearly beloved child of its hope of life or sight. Henri was still speaking.

"What can we do?" he asked. He had already asked the question several times before. "What can we do, Mademoiselle?"

Fleur hesitated a moment, then she knew the answer.

75

"But the answer is easy. We must go tonight."

"Tonight!"—Henri echoed the word stupidly.

Behind him Fleur saw Madame Bouvais straighten herself and stand very still, her face expressionless.

"But of course," Fleur insisted, "what else can we do? Go and fetch Louis and bring your boat to the beach. At the quay you can say you are bringing it round to clean it ready for the inspection tomorrow— make some excuse, you can surely think of one."

"But the coastguard?" Henri asked.

Fleur stared at him, her eyes dark.

"There is only one man on duty at a time—isn't that so? Only one armed, the other inside the hut, perhaps asleep—and there are three of you!"

Henri understood; she saw, too, that her idea had taken hold of him. He was still for a moment, his eyes pensive, his fingers playing idly with a little twig, and as she watched it was as if some machine was beginning to work inside him.

Henri's mind had absorbed her idea and was starting to work on it, was moving quicker ... quicker ... until he grasped it completely and sprang to his feet, his whole face alight.

"You are right, Mademoiselle; it is perfect that way, you will see. You will be ready as soon as it is dark?"

"As soon as it is dark," Fleur repeated.

Henri sped from the kitchen. They heard his footsteps clatter across the yard and fade into the distance. Only then did Fleur look again at Madame Bouvais. She was still standing as if turned to stone.

Now that the moment of parting is upon her, Fleur thought, it is almost unbearable. She moved across the room, put her arms round the older woman and kissed her cheek.

"I'm sorry," she whispered, "so terribly sorry!"

Madame Bouvais turned away, not roughly or rudely as if she refused Fleur's gesture of sympathy, but quietly as if the burden of her sorrow was so great that there was no way in which she could express it in words.

Fleur, carrying Jack's supper down to the cellar, was concerned with her own inner regret. She had somehow looked forward to tonight in her own mind as if it were a celebration. She had planned it as a night when she and Jack must say good-bye to the past and turn towards the future.

And now, in the flood-tide of her love—another change.

"Oh, God!" she prayed suddenly. "Let Jack go on loving me. Don't let me lose him, I need him so!"

She felt her prayer was selfish and yet at the same time she knew that Jack needed her too, needed her in many ways more than she did him.

If she had not come to the farm, perhaps he would have done something stupid, tried to make an escape to soon and been captured, involving himself in desperate consequences and perhaps involving the Bouvais as well.

She had prevented that; she had given him a new strength and a renewed confidence in himself.

She knocked on the partition wall. They had a sign of their own now, a different one from that used by Suzanne and the rest of the family. He knocked his reply, the panel slid back and she carried in his food.

"The same generous choice of soup or soup, I suppose?" Jack asked. "My goodness! It will be fun to have a decent meal for a change. Fancy a nice cut off the joint or a steak!"

"You may have one sooner than you think!"

Jack looked at her sharply.

"What do you mean?"

Fleur told him Henri's news and her own decision which had changed him from despair to elation.

"So we're to go tonight!" Jack exclaimed.

"Yes, we are going tonight." Impossible to prevent her voice from dropping and a slight tremor of the lips.

"But that's marvellous! Now I shan't have to lie awake longing for tomorrow. I couldn't sleep a wink last night, I was so excited, and I was thinking all the

77

time what a state I should be in tonight. Fleur, this is stupendous! We couldn't have better weather for it, just look at that mist!"

"Perfect."

Jack looked at her.

"You didn't sound too pleased. It's all right, isn't it? You aren't keeping anything back from me?"

"I've told you exactly what's happened," she said and smiled at his excitement.

"Perhaps we'll be having breakfast in dear old England. Eggs and bacon! What would you think of that?"

"It sounds all right." In spite of every effort, Fleur knew that her voice sounded flat.

"You're worried." Jack put his arms round her and drew her head against his shoulder. He tipped up her chin, holding it between his fingers. "Don't look anxious, darling. We'll make it all right—we've got to! I've had the luck of the devil all through this war—it isn't going to fail me now."

"Don't boast!" Fleur said quickly.

"I'm not! Besides, I'm touching wood."

He put his hand against the table, then slipped it back against the warm softness of her neck.

"You think we're happy here," he challenged. "Wait until we get to England. We'll be married and I'll show you the real meaning of love."

"I only hope to go on being—as happy."

"You shall," Jack promised, and then he gave out a sudden whoop of excitement. "Just think—tonight! We really start tonight!"

CHAPTER EIGHT

"Jack! Jack!"

"It's all right—drink this."

A gentle voice spoke with authority and a firm hand lifted Fleur's head from the pillow so that she felt her lips touch some cool, revivifying liquid. She opened her eyes. She saw white walls, a calm-faced, white-capped nurse bending over her. A screen at the end of the bed blocked her vision.

She was in hospital, her brain took in the fact: then a voice commanded her—

"You are all right. You are quite safe now. Go to sleep."

She shut her eyes, obedient as a child, and let herself drift away into unconsciousness.

Later, much later, she began to remember, to let all the events and happenings of the past hours come back to her. She saw them clearly in all their agony and suffering, yet without the terror and fear which had been her own most prevailing emotions at the time they had taken place.

Yet despite everything, despite what must have been the almost overwhelming odds, their adventure had succeeded, they had reached home.

At least, three of them had. Louis had died just before they were picked up by a coastal motor-boat.

It was of Louis that Fleur thought most often, even

while she knew that in her dreams she cried out for Jack, longed for him, felt that without his sustaining love and his indomitable courage she could not go on.

For nothing, she felt, could ever erase the memory of Louis's head in her lap, the horror of watching him grow weaker and weaker, of knowing that his life was ebbing away, yet being unable to prevent it.

The whole story of their flight in retrospect seemed almost too fantastic to be credible. As her eyes closed against the soft pillow, Fleur wondered if anyone would believe them, if it was worth telling the story and expecting people to credit what seemed sheer fiction.

She remembered that walk to the boat from the Bouvais farm, the sound of their footsteps although they tried to muffle them by walking on the grass by the side of the road and in the fields. The noise of a stone carelessly kicked was like a pistol shot.

Over and over again Fleur found herself thinking that they were mad to attempt an escape, mad to risk comparative security for what appeared to be certain death.

Yet she knew she was the only one who was afraid. Jack was thrilled and excited, but at the same time outwardly calm, just as she felt he must be when he took off in his aeroplane to fly over the enemy territory. The sense of adventure swept away from him almost all personal feeling.

He was out to do a job, he was determined to make a success of it. The fact that he himself might never complete the course was, Fleur knew, of so little account that he hardly gave it a moment's thought.

Henri was of the same temperament as Jack, but he wasn't so experienced or so practised at disguising his feelings. He was very pale and his dark eyes shone with an unnatural excitement.

He had said his good-byes to his family almost impatiently. Madame Bouvais had been dry-eyed—that in itself had been a surprise. It was Henri's father who held back the slow painful tears with difficulty and was unable to speak when the auctual moment for departure came.

Suzanne had clung to her brother for a little longer than the rest and then with a gesture which was infinitely moving because of its utter simplicity she had said, *"Bon voyage, mon cher,"* and added softly, "long live France."

Yes, Fleur knew that she would find no sympathy for her own regrets and indecision from Jack and Henri. They were men with a purpose, they had for the moment a one-point concentration and nothing else was of interest to them. They were determined to win through; other matters must wait until that had been achieved.

Louis was different. Fleur had only met the slim, dark-haired young man once before and yet she felt almost an affinity with him.

She could tell that he was highly sensitive, driven, she sensed, by an idealism which made him intensely patriotic and engendered in him an almost abnormal hatred for the men who had violated his country.

As they moved in silence through the dark night, Fleur sensed that here was someone with whom she had much in common, a man, too, whose nerves were as taut and vibrating as were her own.

Their plans had been fully laid. Their first objective was the coastguards' hut on the promontory above the beach.

As they got near it, Fleur was left some distance off with the luggage, the food and all that they considered necessary for the voyage.

She had not wanted to go forward with them while they dealt with the coastguards, and yet, when she was left alone, she had felt that nothing could be more terrible than waiting in the soft, misty darkness, not knowing whether anyone would return.

She expected every moment to hear a shot, the sound of raised voices, to learn that help was coming from other Germans on guard near the town.

She listened to intently that she began to imagine

81

sounds. Suddenly she realised that although the night was chilly she was drenched in sweat, her hands clenched until the nails had cut deeply into the palms.

Ten minutes ... a quarter of an hour ... she kept glancing at the luminous figures of Jack's watch which he had given her to hold. Never had time seemed to pass so slowly; it was as if a whole lifetime ticked by between the moment when they left her and that moment, breathless and palpitating, when she heard someone approach. Who was it? Friend or foe?

Then, out of the darkness she heard a whisper.

"Are you there, Fleur?" It was Jack.

"What has happened?" Her voice cracked, she heard her own tones, unnaturally high, unnaturally shrill.

"It's all right. Henri got a nasty knock on the side of the head, but he's all right. Come on."

There was no more to be said. They picked up the luggage and descended slowly and in silence towards the beach ...

It was just as dawn was breaking when the real moment of terror began. They were sighted by a coastal plane returning from patrol. The pilot signalled to them. He swept low over the water circling round to inspect them.

They knew than that he was suspicious—must obviously be suspicious of a boat so far out.

The next thing they knew was that machine-gun bullets were spattering round them, splashing in the water, ripping through the sails. They threw themselves flat and even as they did so Louis gave a little groan.

For a moment none of them dared move ... they lay, holding their breath, motionless in the bottom of the boat ... Then as the plane zoomed away Fleur raised her head and saw what she had most dreaded—a crimson patch spreading over the back of the blue fishing jersey which Louis wore.

To their utter relief the plane did not return. While they tended Louis as best they could with bandages improvised from torn-up handkerchiefs, they held a council among themselves.

"We must alter course. That swine is certain to send a patrol boat out for us."

They made Louis as comfortable as possible. Fleur sat beside him while Henri and Jack swung the boat over, taking her due east for several miles. The day dawned dark and thundery.

Presently the rain teemed down upon them, soaking them all to the skin, and the sea became unpleasantly rough. Fleur was a good sailor, Jack was not. Soon she had two invalids on her hands, although Louis was by far the quieter of the two.

He lay still, only occasionally he shivered and murmured that he was cold. They piled everything they could upon him; finally Fleur took off her own coat to wrap round his legs.

The boat began to ship a certain amount of water. After a time Fleur asked Henri to move Louis so that his head rested in her lap. They had brought some food with them, potatoes, bread, and two bottles of wine.

They made Louis drink some of the wine, forcing it between his lips, but soon he drifted into unconsciousness. He was not in pain, but Fleur had the uneasy feeling that his wound was mortal.

Jack's bouts of seasickness became worse, Fleur herself felt light-headed and dizzy from the continual motion.

It was only Henri who appeared normal, staring ahead as he steered the boat, drenched through and through, his dark hair damp against his forehead, yet seeming impervious to everything except his resolution to get them to safety.

As the light began to fail, they realised that they must spend another night at sea. There was no sign of land and Henri confessed fiercely and with a wealth of explanations and excuses that he had lost his bearings.

"Why haven't we got a compass?" Jack asked, over

and over again, although he knew they had been unable to obtain one.

The motor chugged on. It had slowed down a good deal during the storm, but in the monotonous rise and fall of the waves it went on indomitably.

The night was cold, they shivered without their coats and Louis's forehead was like ice. His hands too seemed to have not only no warmth but no life in them.

Once or twice during the passing hours Fleur drifted into a semi-coma of insensibility. It was nothing so simple as sleep, it was just that her brain was too weary to function further and must rest, if only for a few minutes.

Then she would come back with a start to the realisation that they were still ploughing onwards. Jack was better, although every now and then he was overcome by a ghastly retching.

Up and down, up and down the boat swung, sometimes going so deep into the trough of a wave that it seemed to Fleur they would never rise again, yet always it righted itself.

Once or twice Fleur wondered if human discomfort could stand much more. Her clothes, limp and damp, stuck to her body. She was hungry, conscious of an aching vacuum inside her.

During the storm their bread and potatoes had become soaked with sea-water and were quite uneatable. The last bottle of wine was finished. Fleur found herself thinking of hot coffee, of tea with milk and sugar.

She chided herself for being so trivial and bent over Louis again . . .

It seemed to her that he was hardly breathing. She felt the bandages and knew that they were soaked in blood; she wondered if she ought to change them, but decided she must wait until it was light.

Then, as the dawn came, as the glow in the east enabled her to see clearly, she knew that Louis was dead.

For a long time she sat very still. She did not tell the others. Somehow she could not force the words between

84

her lips. At last, when she felt she must speak, when the burden of her knowledge was too much to be borne alone, she heard Henri give a cry, a cry hoarse and violent.

Turning her head she saw the bow and spray of a motor boat speeding towards them ...

"They've caught us!" she thought, and felt in her utter weariness that death was almost to be desired.

Then she saw that Jack and Henri were waving, shouting, their words incoherent, but the triumph and excitement of their voices clear enough.

"Les Anglais! Les Anglais!"

She saw the tears running down Henri's face, his eyes blazing. Then the whole scene faded; she was alone in a great darkness in which she was conscious of one thing only Louis's head in her lap. . . .

*　　*　　*

Of what happened after that Fleur was always a little hazy.

Later she was to learn that she narrowly escaped pneumonia but in her hospital bed she was content to drift into sleep to escape further questioning. Only as she began to get better did she want Jack.

He came bursting into her room when she was needing him most. It seemed to her at that moment that she would never ask anything else except his smile of welcome, the joy of seeing his outstretched arms, of feeling his lips first on her cheek and then against her lips.

"Darling, are you better? You must hurry up and get well. Everything's fine, the people here have been like angels to us. And what do you think?—my mother's coming down this morning. I'm going to arrange for you to come home with us right away."

"But, Jack, perhaps she won't want that?"

"Of course she will. And what's more, she'll feel jolly proud of us. We're little tin-pot heroes about here, I can tell you. The Mayor himself called on me this morning.

As for Henri, he's got instructions to report at once to General de Gaulle's headquarters. He's as pleased as if they'd already made him an admiral."

"And ... and Louis?"

The gaiety died from Jack's face.

"Louis was buried yesterday."

"Poor Louis! And yet I don't know, perhaps he's escaped completely ... more than we have. I didn't know him well, but I felt somehow he was the type who would always suffer in one way or another."

"Good heavens! What made you think of that?" Jack asked. "He seemed to me an ordinary sort of chap. Nice though. I'm damned sorry about it."

Fleur said no more. She could not explain her feelings to Jack. She had the strange idea that Louis had paid for them, for their safety, for their lives. It was as if a sacrifice had been demanded and Louis had been content that he personally should ensure their freedom.

She was taken in an ambulance to Jack's home and made comfortable in a small, tastefully decorated bedroom overlooking the garden.

Jack's mother lived in a suburb outside the town of Melford. The house, built in the last twenty years, was light and airy, and, Fleur was soon to learn, tidy with a neat punctiliousness which one would expect to irritate any normal man.

Perhaps the late Mr. Reynolds had liked such tidiness; anyway, it was certainly irksome to his son in spite of the fact that Jack was the one person who was allowed to scatter his things round and go unrebuked, although his mother quickly tidied up after him.

Mrs. Reynolds reminded Fleur irresistibly of Mrs. Tittlemouse in the Beatrice Potter books which she had read as a child. Mrs. Tittlemouse was a field-mouse who spent her entire time keeping her house clean, going round with a pan and brush after anyone had walked on her floors with dirty feet.

Mrs. Reynolds was small, sandy-haired, and, as Fleur's Nannie would have said, "as neat as a new pin".

Her house was polished, cleaned and dusted until every piece of furniture shone with an almost supernatural brightness; in fact—again to quote one of Nannie's pronouncements—"one could eat one's food off the floor".

Why one should want to do so Fleur had never fathomed, but she quite understood after staying a few days with Mrs. Reynolds that here was the one house where such an action would not be revolting.

Plates, vases, ornaments, glasses, cups and saucers had their own little mats lest they should spoil the polish of the table; even the ash-trays were hardly allowed to contain a piece of ash for more than a few moments before they were emptied.

The whole place was spick and span, and if Mrs. Reynolds had an interest outside the walls of Ivy Dene, it was hard to know what it was.

Mollie, Jack's sister, did not resemble her mother physically, but she was not unlike her in temperament. She too had a tidy mind which put people in categories and seldom allowed them to emerge from the particular pigeonhole to which they were first apportioned.

Fleur felt a reserve and what amounted almost to dislike in the atmosphere, although Mollie's manner towards her was punctiliously correct and polite.

Fleur, sitting in the drawing-room on her second day downstairs, heard Mollie come in at the front door, put her umbrella in the rack and enter the room.

Mrs. Reynolds had been knitting and turning the heel of a sock, doing so, Fleur noticed, with much neatness and at an even, unhurried rate of progress. It was impossible to imagine Mrs. Reynolds dropping a stitch, she would never be so inexact.

Jack had gone out to play golf, and Fleur, longing to go with him but knowing that it would prove too arduous, had felt resentful that, smiling and healthy, he must go off without her while she sat at home.

Mollie came into the drawing-room now. She was taking off her gloves, blowing into each one as she did so to straighten the fingers.

"So you're back, dear," Mrs. Reynolds said somewhat obviously. "Did you get the cotton I wanted?"

"Yes, and your needles as well," Mollie replied. "And who do you think I met at the post office?"

"I can't think."

"Nancy Travers." Mollie's pale voice for once held something of a dramatic quality.

Mrs. Reynold's knitting dropped in her lap.

"So she's back."

Mollie nodded.

"Yes, and she asked after Jack. She's coming round to see him this evening."

"Did she . . . did she say anything else?"

"No, and I didn't volunteer any information," Mollie replied.

Mother and daughter looked at each other somewhat strangely, Fleur thought.

"I'll go and take off my hat," Mollie added.

She left the room. Mrs. Reynolds picked up her knitting. There had been nothing unusual in the conversation, yet Fleur had the uneasy feeling that there was something important which she had missed or not understood.

"Who is Nancy Travers?" she asked at length.

For a moment Mrs. Reynolds looked startled, as if she had forgotten that Fleur was there. Then her thin lips pursed, she seemed to hesitate before anwering firmly, without raising her eyes from her knitting:

"Nancy Travers? Haven't you heard us speak of her before? She is the girl to whom Jack is engaged."

CHAPTER NINE

"But, darling, you must understand!" Jack said. "Can't you see my point of view?"

"No, I can't," Fleur replied. "You were engaged to this girl morally even if it wasn't formally announced. You knew that and you could at least have been honest with me—have told me about her."

"Why should I?" Jack asked. "Can't you see that it meant nothing at the time. We drifted into the engagement when we were kids. Oh, I suppose we took it seriously to a certain extent, but Mother disapproved of her and so did Mollie."

"All the same you were engaged," Fleur insisted.

"Well, if you like to call it that," Jack said restlessly. "Besides, if I'd told you, would it have made all that amount of difference?"

Fleur hesitated. She tried to be honest with herself. She had a horror, an ingrained repugnance, of taking away another woman's man.

Those years in which she had known of Sylvia's infidelity to her father had left their mark upon her; there was and always would be something unpleasant in being made love to by a man who was legally or morally attached to someone else.

"Can't you understand?" she asked Jack passionately over and over again.

But he wouldn't admit it even while she guessed that

deep within himself he was ashamed of his behaviour.

"It didn't seem to matter over there," he said pathetically; and with that she agreed.

Living on the farm they had seemed to be isolated, to be in a world of their own in which nothing conventional, nothing of commonplace, ordinary, everyday life could affect them.

But how often had he thought of Nancy, she wondered. How often, when he was kissing her, had his mind wandered towards this other girl who loved him too?

She could not forgive him, could not forget that moment in the drawing-room when his mother's words had turned her heart to ice and made her feel that once again the whole world as she knew it was crashing about her ears.

If she had not been so bitterly hurt and wounded within herself, she might have found a genuine pity for Jack. As so many other men had been before him, he was torn between two loves.

Later, when she saw Nancy, she understood. She was the fragile, clinging sort of girl who will always make an appeal to the virile, stalwart young man. She was shrewd and amusing in a somewhat suburban way and despite her appearance was doubtless very strong.

But she was the type who would always be protected and cosseted, the type which men have regarded as "the little woman" since the beginning of creation, the type, too, who having once got a man will seldom let him go.

With her first sight of Nancy, Fleur knew that the die was cast.

She had already told herself that she must leave the Reynolds household, that she must forget Jack; and yet she still half-played with the idea, hoping against hope that it would not be necessary, that her love was stronger than anything else.

In the summer-house Jack had begged her to let things drift, at any rate for the moment.

"Why should we say anything?" he asked. "I owe

Nancy no explanation and anyway, for the moment, there's no question of my marrying anyone. I told you that I must wait. Besides, in this precarious life, what's the point of leaving a widow behind?"

The hard bitterness of his words made Fleur cry out. "Don't talk like that," she begged.

But she knew that even while he could still hurt her because he talked of dying, he was prevaricating, playing for time, trying to evade the consequences of his own actions.

More than once she longed to say to him: "Why don't you stop being frightened? You can't run away from life. You are running now from me, from Nancy, even from your mother."

But she knew Jack would not understand. He had never been brought up to think of anything save that which was superficial and commonplace.

He ate his meals, played his games of golf, cricket and football, he slept when he was tired, and he read the papers to learn what other people were thinking and feeling; but he managed personally never to think or feel beyond a certain point. Jack had never suffered mentally.

But the knowledge of all this did not help her personally. Over and over again she found herself sobbing his name into the darkness, aching and yearning for him with all the force of her being.

"I love you," she whispered. "Oh, Jack, I love you so!"

She had been so sure of his love, sure because of the certainty within her own heart. Now she knew that the premonition she had had when she left France, that she was going not towards happiness but away from it, had been correct.

"I can't bear it!" Fleur said more than once. "First Lucien and now Jack." For it was indeed as though Jack too had died when her illusion of him had crashed and fallen.

She wondered if she would have the strength to resist

if he were to cast all caution aside and beg her to marry him now and at once. Though she knew that much of her idealism had been shattered, yet one part of her mind still loved him overwhelmingly.

"I should want to refuse," Fleur thought, "but I believe I should never have the courage or the good sense."

When she came down to breakfast the following morning, Jack had already left the house. It had been arranged that he should play in a golf match at a course some twenty miles away.

Mrs. Reynolds had nearly finished breakfast. Fleur helped herself to coffee and a minute piece of bacon and then, just before her hostess left the table, asked:

"Don't you think I might go to the Labour Exchange this morning and try to get some work?"

"Do you really want some?" Mrs. Reynolds asked. "I thought you heard from your bank yesterday."

"I did," Fleur answered, "and I have some money there waiting for me. I suppose I could go on living a life of leisure, at least for a little while; but I prefer to work, although I doubt if I should be strong enough to enter one of the women's services at the moment."

"I'm quite certain you won't be able to do that," Mrs. Reynolds said. "In fact, I was speaking of it to the doctor only yesterday."

Fleur felt this remark was revealing. So already Mrs. Reynolds had considered getting rid of the unwanted guest that her son had brought to the house.

"What did the doctor say?" she asked.

"He said that you would have to take life slowly for at least three months," Mrs. Reynolds replied. "I should imagine, however, that an office job might be permissible."

"I think the best thing would be for me to go the Labour Exchange and have a talk with them."

"It's a very good idea," Mrs. Reynolds agreed. "Would you like me to go with you?"

"I'd rather go alone," Fleur replied, and Mrs. Reynolds nodded as if it was what she expected.

The interviewer at the Labour Exchange was sympathetic and understanding. It was a small local office and Fleur found that the woman to whom she talked had already heard of her and Jack's adventures.

She repeated what the doctor had said about her joining the services, but remarked that, of course, she was quite prepared to bring a certificate or have an examination should they wish it.

"That won't be necessary, Miss Garton," the woman in charge said. "We quite understand the circumstances; in fact, I think it marvellous of you to come here so soon. I wonder you aren't grey-haired after all you've been through. Why, it sounds just like a film story!"

Fleur smiled bitterly, and then, before she could prevent the words, they slipped out.

"Without the conventional happy ending?"

The woman looked embarrassed and she guessed that there was already speculation as to whether or not she would marry Jack.

"Well, at least I've given them something to talk about," Fleur thought.

"You'd like a local job, of course?"

Fleur shook her head.

"No, I don't want to stay in Melford . . ."

"That's a pity, because I have something here which I think might suit you."

"What is it?" Fleur asked. She was determined, whatever was offered, to get away from Melford, away from Jack and from all that would keep him irresistibly in her mind.

"Well, of course, it might not be the type of thing you'd care for; it's only a suggestion, but in your present state of health you wouldn't want anything too hard and this sounds easy."

"What is it?" Fleur asked again.

"It's the post of housekeeper-companion."

"To a woman?"

"But of course," was the answer in a somewhat reproving tone. "And quite an important personage as it happens. We have been asked to make discreet inquiries about finding someone; but I feel that if you'd take it, you would be so suitable that I might mention to you the name of the inquirer."

"Well, who is it?"

"Mrs. Mitcham, mother of Sir Norman Mitcham. Of course, you know who he is."

"Head of Mitcham Motors," Fleur said.

She recalled the conversation with Jack when they had talked of Norman Mitcham and his works. What had Jack said about him?—"He's like a juggernaut."

"I might consider it," she said slowly. "Could I see Mrs. Mitcham."

"I could make an appointment for you to go to Greystone Priory—that is Sir Norman's house, you know. It's about five miles from here but a bus passes the drive gates."

"I think I'd like an interview."

She felt suddenly curious about Sir Norman Mitcham and his mother. She did not know why; it was just that snatches of the conversation which she had had with Jack came back to her.

There was something rather fascinating about the story of the great works built up from a very small beginning—the works where Jack had been employed before the war. How he loved engines! She remembered how his face lit up when he spoke of them.

"Would you be able to go this afternoon?"

Fleur recalled her thoughts with a jerk.

"Yes . . . yes, I'd like to go as soon as possible."

"If you will excuse me, I'll see if that would be convenient."

Fleur waited.

After all, there's no harm in being interviewed, she thought. If I don't like the job, I needn't take it. If I do, well, it's far enough from Jack and his mother for them not to trouble me unduly. Anyway, Jack will be going away soon.

She felt her heart give a throb of dismay at the prospect. Going back to his Squadron! Was she never to see his face again, never to know the joy of feeling his arms round her, the bliss of his lips clinging to hers? From the past she heard her own voice, passionate, deep and low, asking:

"You love me? You do love me, Jack? We'll never leave each other, will we? We'll always go on loving each other like this?"

And Jack's reply, murmured against her neck,

"You're so beautiful! I'll always love you, always, all my life."

How easily love could be set aside by other things, by the familiarity of people and places, by games and work, by being in another environment.

She looked up to see the woman returning to her. She was smiling.

"Mrs. Mitcham will be pleased to see you at three o'clock this afternoon, Miss Garton."

CHAPTER TEN

Fleur walked slowly up the drive leading to Greystone
Priory.

Every now and then she stopped to rest, feeling not
tired, but weak about the legs, and at times overcome
by a slight giddiness which, however, soon passed. She
felt as if she was taking part in another adventure, for
she had not told the Reynolds where she was going that
afternoon.

The bus had carried her, as she had been told, to the
stone gates of Greystone Priory. As they had left the
suburbs of Melford behind, she had seen in the distance
the vast factory of the Mitcham works.

It was not actually on the road they took from the
town, but it covered such a vast area that it was conspicuous a long way off. It was, of course, camouflaged;
but even so the many long buildings, stretching out like
the arms of an octopus, covered acres of the flat land to
the south of the town. Fleur looked at it with interest.

Then all signs of factories and of town life were left
behind and they were in the open country, green and
exceedingly beautiful in the summer sunshine, the only
reminder of war an occasional searchlight site or an
army lorry parked by the roadside.

The drive curved, and at the end of it Fleur saw the
Priory. She gave an involuntary exclamation, for it was
more beautiful than anything she had anticipated.

Somehow, although the name sounded ancient, she had expected Norman Mitcham to live in a new, or at least a somewhat pretentious house.

The Priory, of grey stone, was low and rambling. Architecturally it must have been contributed to by many successive generations, but Fleur guessed the original structure was very old indeed, perhaps fifteenth-century.

It had an almost unearthly loveliness after the pseudo-Tudor and bright stucco of Melford's suburbia. The warm, weather-beaten bricks, the ogived Gothic windows with their small panes of iridescent glass, the gables, the ancient tiled roof, and the chimneys, elegant and graceful, many of Tudor origin, made a picture which was essentially and characteristically English.

It was not only the house itself which had such charm, there was its setting.

Almost at the foot of the front door stretched a small lake surrounded by a grey stone balustrade; on it black swans moved slowly, making the pale grey of the walls seem even paler; the blue sky was reflected in the water and the sunshine shimmered upon it like mirrored magic.

Behind the house there was the dark, verdant green of fir trees, planted to make both a background and a protective wall as the setting to a priceless jewel.

Fleur stood very still for some time, just looking.

"It's lovely!" she thought over and over again. Then she set forth once more with a new and gladdening interest, half-decided already that she would like to live at the Priory.

The interior, on first impressions, was as lovely as the exterior.

The butler led her through the hall furnished with heavy, and what Fleur felt must be priceless, pieces of furniture—polished walnut, carved oak—and everywhere pictures which even the most uneducated would guess to be masterpieces.

Sir Norman Mitcham certainly has taste, Fleur thought, and wondered how he had acquired it.

She was shown into a small but exquisitely furnished room and was asked to wait. The tapestry-covered chairs, the sofas of ancient velvet and the curtains which had been embroidered generations ago were in keeping with the panelled walls of dark oak on which hung gilt-framed pictures.

"I never anticipated anything like this," Fleur thought.

Looking through the window she saw a rose garden built round an old sundial, and behind it a broad grass walk such as the Georgians loved, with a Grecian temple in the distance.

"This place must surely be famous," she ruminated, and tried to remember if amongst her father's books she had ever seen a picture of it.

"Greystone Priory," she repeated to herself. Vaguely it seemed to her that it had a familiar ring, and yet whatever she had known or heard of it eluded her.

"Will you come this way, Miss, please?"

She turned to see the butler waiting for her in the doorway, an old man, pompous and portly, with one of those inscrutable expressions from which one could learn nothing.

She followed him out into the hall and up the broad oak staircase where the newels supported heraldic leopards holding shields between their paws. They went along a wide gallery, soft-carpeted and hung with portraits; then a door was opened and she heard her own name announced in stentorian tones.

"Miss Garton, Madam."

She stood in the doorway, irresolute, surprised at what she saw. The room was large; one side of it seemed to be composed entirely of windows; and where there were no windows there were mirrors, so that the whole effect was one of light.

At the far end of the room was a huge four-poster bed hung with crimson brocade, surmounted by great waving fronds of ostrich feathers, and in the bed, propped up by many cushions, was the most amazing old woman Fleur had ever seen in her life.

She was obviously very old, for her face was furrowed with wrinkles and her mouth sunk and withered; but she wore on her head a wig of brilliant copper-coloured curls, dressed high in the fashion made popular by Queen Alexandra.

There was a lace shawl round her shoulders; beneath it one could see a tulle bow tied coyly round her raddled neck; and on her hands, clawlike with age, the knuckles red and swollen with rheumatism, she wore a large number of rings.

Sapphires, rubies, diamonds and emeralds all sparkled and were reflected in the innumerable mirrors as she waved her hand towards Fleur, inviting her to come nearer.

"Come in, my dear," she said, in a voice which seemed to have some dry, humorous quality about it. "Come in and sit down. My son said he would be back to meet you, but of course he's late. It's what we have to expect these days, unpunctuality and incivility—but then—war altogether is a damned nuisance, don't you think so?"

Fleur felt as if she had no adequate answer for such a question; she murmured something in reply, and feeling gauche and rather stupid, she moved towards the bed and sat down in the chair pushed forward for her by the butler.

On closer inspection the old lady was even more fantastic than she had been in the distance, for her face was powdered almost dead-white and she had drawn in her eyebrows heavily with a dark pencil.

Fleur could see now that she wore two fine pear-shaped diamonds in her ears and that, half pushed up her arm, under the sleeves of a pink woollen bed-jacket worn beneath the ancient lace shawl, there glittered the fine stones of a magnificent diamond bracelet.

The bedspread was also of lace, old lace backed with

a soft satin, but there was little of it to be seen; the bed was strewn with papers of all sorts, books and boxes, magazines and—Fleur noted with amusement—fashion papers.

She sat down, aware that the old lady's eyes, bright and penetrating, were watching her every movement.

"You can go, Barham," she said sharply to the butler who was still hovering in the background.

"Very good, Madam." He went out, shutting the door almost silently behind him.

"Now stop looking surprised," Mrs. Mitcham commanded Fleur, "and tell me about yourself."

"Was I? I . . . I'm sorry," Fleur stammered, nonplussed and embarrassed.

"Oh, don't be sorry," the old lady said with a chuckle. "Most people are surprised when they first see me, but they get used to me. One can get used to anything in time, and anyway I can assure you I'm far better than the average old woman with her knitting, her parrot and her condemnation of everything that's young and attractive. Do you enjoy life?"

"I try to," Fleur said.

She felt that this interview was more amazing than anything she had anticipated in her wildest dreams.

"So I should hope at your age! Well, I enjoy it too, and I don't intend to have people around me who pull long faces and expect me to do likewise because I've got one foot in the grave. I'm not quite dead yet and, until I am, I intend to enjoy myself. Now tell me about your escape from France."

"You've heard about it, then?"

"Of course, of course. They told me at the Labour Exchange. Quite bucked up they were, to have something interesting to offer me for a change. Mealy-mouthed parsons' daughters and decayed gentlewomen who only want the situation if they can bring their ancient pug are the usual applicants they suggest.

"Oh, yes, they told me all about you, but I want to

hear your version—aren't you going to marry the young man?"

Fleur found herself blushing, she was not certain why, but the sudden and unexpected reference to Jack made the colour flood in a crimson tide over her neck and cheeks. Mrs. Mitcham chuckled.

"Touched a tender spot, have I?"

"I'm not going to marry Mr. Reynolds," Fleur said quickly. "In fact, he's engaged to someone else."

She tried to speak with indifference, but somehow she felt as if the old woman guessed the truth.

"And so you're looking for a job," she remarked dryly. "Well, do you think I'd suit you?"

"Surely it's the other way round?" Fleur replied gently.

"I made up my mind as soon as you walked into the room," Mrs. Mitcham answered. "When I saw you I thought, 'That's the girl for me—pretty, attractive, has character and ought to be able to stand up to being bullied twenty-four hours a day'."

"Will you bully me?" Fleur asked, smiling.

"Of course. I bully everyone, including my son, although he likes to pretend that I don't. Good gracious me! If one can't get one's own way when one's over seventy, when can one? I've had a hard life one way and another and I'm making up for it now.

"If it weren't for these damn fools of doctors I'd be on my legs gadding about; but they know nothing, so here I am, bedridden, but determined to enjoy it. Yes, you'll suit me all right."

At that moment the door opened and Fleur looked round to see a man enter. She knew at once that this must be Sir Norman Mitcham and was immediately conscious of a sense of disappointment.

After the house and the fantastic appearance of his mother she had instinctively anticipated someone unusual or at least distinguished. Norman Mitcham was neither.

Of medium height, he had somewhat ordinary features and dark hair which was touched with grey at the temples. He looked like hundreds of other men one sees going to business in every industrial town in the country.

His clothes were as unnoticeable as he was himself. It was only his eyes that were in anyway exceptional, for they were dark grey and very perceptive.

When he spoke one noticed the firmness of his jaw and the hard, almost harsh lines at the side of his mouth. He spoke in a quiet manner, but with a force that was somehow disturbing and slightly repellent.

"I told Barham that Miss Garton was to wait until I arrived," he said abruptly.

"I said I'd like to see her," his mother replied.

"That doesn't excuse Barham for disobeying my orders. I've told him, if this sort of thing happens again, he will have to go."

Mrs. Mitcham snorted irreverently.

"You know he's been here forty years. To get rid of Barham you'd have to burn down the house."

"Well, I'll burn it down then," Sir Norman said, "but I will be obeyed."

He spoke quietly and there was no rise or fall in the cadence of his tones, and yet somehow Fleur felt that he was not being dramatic or absurd. He expected obedience and he would get it.

There was a cool ruthlessness in his manner which she disliked intensely. Slowly she got to her feet.

"I am sorry," she said, "if I am the cause of any trouble."

Sir Norman walked across the room to her and held out his hand.

"How do you do? My mother is not to be tired by doing too much—those are the doctor's orders and mine."

"The only thing that tires me is being bored," Mrs. Mitcham interposed. "I have engaged Miss Garton, so really you needn't have bothered to come back. You could have spent the afternoon in the factory—you know you'd prefer that."

"I think it would be advisable for me to have a talk with Miss Garton before anything is decided," Sir Norman said quietly.

"Well, take her downstairs then, take her away, but don't forget I want her. She'd better come tomorrow. No point in waiting, especially"—smirked at Fleur—"if that young man of yours is engaged to someone else."

Fleur, conscious of Sir Norman's eyes upon her, felt her cheeks flame again at this last remark, and yet despite her embarrassment she liked Mrs. Mitcham, liked her as much as she already disliked Sir Norman. There was a warmth and a humanity about the old woman with her incredible appearance and common voice which was not to be found in her son.

As Fleur walked with him along the passage and down the stairs she told herself that if she had met him first she would not for a moment have considered the post. Yet she had already made up her mind that she would come to Greystone Priory.

The mere idea of being housekeeper-companion had sounded drab and uninteresting, but here was something quite different, something out of the ordinary and the conventional, which attracted her despite the difficulties she already half-surmised.

She went with Sir Norman into the Library, a room lined from floor to ceiling with books where a huge desk, covered with papers and telephones, told her that this was his own private sanctum.

He pointed to a hard chair opposite the desk and invited her to sit on it and then, abrupt as he seemed to be in everything, he asked for her particulars. Name ... age ... where she had lived before the war ... where she was staying now. She answered his inquiries quietly, yet conscious all the time of an inner resentment.

"He's making it very clear that my position is that of a servant," she thought. "I expect the next thing will be that he'll ask for my references."

Almost as if he had read her thoughts Sir Norman looked across the desk at her and said:

"I'm not going to ask for references even if you wish to give them to me. I pride myself on being able to judge a man or woman at an interview and I prefer to use that judgment rather than rely on the conclusions reached by someone else."

Fleur said nothing; then after a moment, as if he had waited for her reply, he went on:

"I don't know whether my mother has told you what is required. I imagine not—she's not very practical in these matters. I want someone to be a companion to her and also to act as housekeeper.

"By that I do not imply that you need order the food—we have a cook who has been with us many years and does that adequately—but I would like you to act as hostess when I entertain, to keep up a certain authority in the household, and to engage those servants whom I have not time to see myself."

Fleur felt her heart sink. There was something about being asked to act hostess for this man that frightened her; at the same time, however, the house itself called her and overruled her fears. To be hostess in such surroundings! What woman, if she loved lovely things, could ask more of life? Quickly she made her reply.

"I should be willing to do that."

"Then that's settled," Sir Norman said. "Can you come at once?"

"Do you mean today or tomorrow?" Fleur asked, startled.

"I mean what I have said," Sir Norman replied. "I would like you to come now. My mother has been alone too long. Her appearance belies her, she is very frail and yet she has a natural zest for life. The doctors are anxious that she should be kept amused and interested without making the slightest physical exertion. That is not always easy."

"I suppose I can start at once," Fleur said doubtfully. "I should have to go back and get my luggage."

"I will send you in the car," Sir Norman walked across the room and rang the bell. "Your salary will be a hundred a year. Will that be sufficient?"

"Oh, yes, quite."

Barham opened the door.

"Have a car brought round for Miss Garton. She will be fetching her luggage," Sir Norman said. "She will occupy the tapestry room on the first floor and use the sitting-room opening out of it."

"Yes, Sir Norman."

"And kindly inform the household that Miss Garton will be in charge and that all questions that are not referred to me are to be taken to her. Is that understood?"

"Perfectly, Sir Norman."

"Very good." Sir Norman walked across the room, held out his hand to Fleur and as she shook it remarked: "I shall see you this evening then."

Without another word he walked away. Fleur felt he might have added something about her being happy or comfortable.

When she was left alone she stood feeling suddenly afraid, as if she had set in motion a course of action of which she could not possibly see the consequences.

For the last hour or so, while she had been actively engaged in a quick sequence of events, she had forgotten him, but now the memory was close upon her and she could not escape.

It overwhelmed her—the agonising remembrance of those moments when they had been so happy, and all that was most tender had gone out towards him, had encircled him and drawn him close into her arms and heart.

Never again! She could not bear to face the truth of that, she could not bear to realise that Jack, like other people she had loved and lost, must now belong to the past, never to the future or the present.

"I shall have to say good-bye to him," she told herself. Then she remembered that he would not be back until late, perhaps after dinner.

It is best this way, she thought, best to go without saying good-bye. Whatever we said, whatever we felt would still only be an echo of the real thing, of the passion and the tenderness which once was ours.

It was easy to think like that, but far more difficult to suit one's actions to the thought.

She felt the tears start to her eyes, she had a wild impulse to go back on her words, to find Sir Norman and tell him that she could not come tonight. She felt she must have one more evening with Jack, just a few more hours in which she would find a little satisfaction, if only a little, in knowing that physically he was close to her—and yet what was the point?

. Restlessly, Fleur got to her feet.

"I've got to learn to hate him," she thought, "to hate all men, to dispense with love—forget about it. This petty suffering of mine doesn't really matter. Look at this house! The people who have lived in it, who loved and suffered, who were happy or fearful, have gone. Only the house remains. Life is a little thing, transitory and unimportant. How insignificant we are!"

She stood at the window and looked out over the garden. She was conscious of the tears brimming over on to her cheeks, of an aching heart and the quick throbbing of her pulses. The garden was very still and very lovely.

"Please, God, let me find peace here," she prayed.

CHAPTER ELEVEN

Fleur's first days at Greystone Priory passed like a dream.

It was difficult for her to sort out her impressions, but nevertheless the beauty and the atmosphere of the Priory itself gripped her; it was a never failing source of joy and interest.

And despite her own chaotic emotions, which would not let her rest, Fleur did find a certain peace in her environment.

At present it was only superficial, but she acknowledged even that relief gratefully, hoping that finally it would percolate into her consciousness and she would become an integral part of it.

Yet how could she be anything but disturbed and distraught when from the moment she had left the Reynolds household she had been bombarded with letters and telephone calls from Jack?

In her new conception of him and in the disappointment of her love she had somehow believed that he would not mind her going. But the moment she was gone, he realised what he was losing.

The very evening of her arrival she had been fetched to the telephone about nine o'clock.

"What is this I hear?" Jack asked, and his voice was angry. "Mother tells me that you have taken a situation. It can't be true!"

"But it is," Fleur replied. "Why should you be so surprised? I couldn't possibly go on staying with your mother after . . ."

"Don't be so ridiculous!" Jack said. "You know I want you here. Why, I have another week's leave for one thing, and Fleur . . . Fleur, my sweet, you can't leave me like this."

His voice softened; she steeled herself to withstand the appeal in it.

"Please, Jack, be sensible! I left you a little note—you will find it on your dressing-table."

"What does it say?"

"Good-bye."

"But you can't go like this." He was shouting again now.

"I can and I must," Fleur replied, her voice desperate, "and I can't stay talking here—it's too difficult. Good-bye . . . my darling."

She could not help the last endearment, it slipped out, and without waiting for his reply she replaced the receiver, conscious that she was trembling and that she was not far from tears.

She went back to Mrs. Mitcham's bedroom where she had been talking to the old lady when Barham told her that she was wanted on the telephone.

As she reached the door she made an effort to pull herself together, to look normal, but the sharp eyes of her employer missed nothing.

"It's that young man, I'll be bound," the old lady said; and as Fleur did not reply, she continued, "You think you're as miserable as hell, and I wouldn't mind betting he's not worth one tear from your pretty eyes. You take my advice, my dear, and forget him. There's just as good fish in the sea as ever came out."

She chuckled, and there was something obscene in her laughter, Fleur thought; and then as she sat down by the bedside in silence, irritated by this intrusion into her intimate affairs, Mrs. Mitcham suddenly put out a bejewelled hand and covered hers.

"Don't be unhappy, my child. You'll find that most things work out for the best in the long run. That's cold comfort when your heart's bleeding, but you'll live to know I'm speaking the truth."

There was something so kindly in the tone of her voice that Fleur felt the tears spring to her eyes and this time she could not control them.

"There, there," Mrs. Mitcham said. "I'm a tactless old body, but you've got to take me as you find me, for I'm too old to change. Tell me about it—it'll do you good to talk. You've bottled up your feelings until they are in danger of exploding."

And, incredibly it seemed to Fleur, she did tell her.

Afterwards she wondered why, wondered if it was just her own weakness and the usual feminine desire to confide in someone sympathetic, or whether Mrs. Mitcham, despite all her idiosyncrasies, had a unique gift of inviting confidences and receiving them.

Later Fleur was to learn that the latter was the case. All sorts and conditions of people confided in Mrs. Mitcham; there was hardly a human problem, a love affair or trouble of any sort in the household that was not ultimately brought to her.

One of the reasons was her inexhaustible and unfailing interest in humanity. She thrived, and at times, it seemed to Fleur, was kept alive on her curiosity. Nothing was too petty or too trivial to interest her.

Too old to play an active part in life, she lived it second-hand and the vagaries of people were to her a never-failing excitement.

She had, Fleur discovered, suffered from a series of what she called "mealy-mouthed" women. They had been scandalised at her behaviour, shocked to the core of their genteel beings by the coarseness of her utterances.

At first Fleur wondered where she had learnt such expressions until Mrs. Mitcham enlightened her. They were talking about the Priory one afternoon, Fleur saying how beautiful she thought it was, to add in all sincerity:

"It must make up to you for everything, even for being bedridden, to live among such beautiful surroundings."

"If you believe that, you'll believe anything," Mrs. Mitcham said scathingly. "Do you suppose I wouldn't rather have my legs than all the fine fandangles in the world? Besides, I was never impressed by marble halls and all the glitter of gentleman's houses. Give me a nice, wide, polished bar under my elbows and the talk and good humour of the tap-room. That's what I like—that's where I belong."

Fleur turned to look at her with wide eyes. Mrs. Mitcham laughed.

"Didn't they tell you?" she asked. "I thought that bit of gossip would have got round to you. Oh, yes, I was a barmaid—and not ashamed of it either. I don't mind telling you I was the toast of the town in my young days. And then Albert Mitcham comes along and takes me out of it.

"Often thought I was a fool to have married him—might just as well have had my fun and let him drift away like the others. But, no! Nothing would suit him but marriage, and in those days I thought the world well lost for love."

"Perhaps it is," Fleur said.

"Still thinking of that young jackanapes?" Mrs. Mitcham asked.

She seldom spoke of Jack without some term of abuse and Fleur had ceased to mind. Now that she had given her employer her full confidence, she understood how beneath a rough exterior and a tart tongue was a heart full of real sympathy for anyone who was unhappy.

"You forget him—and quickly."

Fleur smiled.

"It's easier said than done," she replied. "You know that."

"I do, and I often regret the hours I've spent weeping for something that couldn't be helped. I'll fight and struggle against things that can be altered; but when a thing's inevitable you've just got to accept it. Besides, he wasn't worthy of you."

"And yet I still want him," Fleur said miserably. "He's gone now—gone back to his Squadron, and every night I find myself thinking what an idiot I was not to see him before he went. He came here one afternoon, did you know that?"

"I did," Mrs. Mitcham replied.

There was little that she didn't know, Fleur thought. The servants all acted as her informants and Barham was certain to have mentioned that Jack had called.

"I felt I couldn't speak about it at the time," Fleur went on. "I behaved like a Victorian schoolgirl, shut myself in my room and refused to come out."

"Afraid of yourself, of course," Mrs. Mitcham commented.

"Exactly. Now I'm ashamed. Jack wouldn't have understood. He came up to say good-bye and I expect to make one last appeal for us to let things drift, to make no decision one way or another about the future."

"And you hadn't the guts to tell him to his face that you'd already made up your mind never to see him again."

"I was afraid that if I saw him I should throw myself into his arms."

"Yes, it's the sort of thing you would do," the old lady cackled. "You're eaten up with sentiment, that's what's wrong with you, my girl, and you can't control your own heart."

"I admit it all," Fleur replied, and her tone was not light, but weary, as if she was utterly tired of herself.

"Forget him," Mrs. Mitcham said again sharply. "Forget him altogether; don't think about him and we won't talk about him. From now on his name won't pass my lips and blast the son of a bitch for making you unhappy!"

Fleur had to laugh.

"You oughtn't to talk like that," she said. "What would the Melford people—who look on your son as so important—think if they could hear some of the things his mother says?"

"Do them the world of good," Mrs. Mitcham replied. "Besides, they don't think he's important. They remember far too well when he was bootboy here in this very house."

"Bootboy!" Fleur exclaimed.

"Yes, that's how he started life. Albert was at sea and I was sharing a house with a married sister. A narrow, parsimonious sort of woman whom I never got on with, but I had to go somewhere, and while I was looking for a house and a job Annie took me in and young Norman."

"Oh, do tell me more about it," Fleur cried as the old lady stopped.

"Getting interested in young Norman?" his mother asked sharply.

"You needn't be frightened of that," Fleur answered quietly.

"I'm not frightened in the way you mean," Mrs. Mitcham said. "If Norman would become a normal human man, I think I'd go down on my knees, creaky though they are, and thank the Almighty."

"What do you mean? Why is he strange? In what way?"

"Oh, it isn't really his fault. He wasn't always quite as bad as this. He was always one for ideas, for taking up a thing and becoming so absorbed in it he could think of nothing else. He was a studious sort of lad, but even so he wouldn't have been inhuman if it hadn't been for Cynthia."

"Cynthia?" Fleur asked. "Who is she?"

"My daughter-in-law," was the surprising answer.

"Do tell me everything from the beginning," Fleur begged. "Do you know, I knew nothing about this. I'd no idea that Sir Norman was married."

112

"He isn't now," Mrs. Mitcham answered grimly. "He divorced the woman. And not before it was time."

"Did he mind? Was he unhappy?"

"Unhappy!" Mrs. Mitcham echoed scornfully. "How could he expect to be anything else, marrying out of his class and out of station and all because he fell in love with a house."

"With a house?" Fleur questioned, bewildered.

"This house, Cynthia's house. He married her because he wanted it—at least, that's always been my belief—and when he got it and Cynthia as well, he found he was about as much at home as a crow let loose in a cage of humming-birds."

"Was Cynthia Lord Granton's daughter?" Fleur asked, gradually beginning to see the story take shape before her eyes.

"Exactly. His only child. The house was left to her when he died, with about as much money to keep it up as would allow her to employ a charwoman twice a week. And there was Norman, making money hand over fist, in the next field so to speak, crazy about the Priory and, so far as everyone knew, crazy about Cynthia too.

"At any rate, she married him. I never set eyes on her until after they were married. I wasn't seeing much of Norman then, he was going up in the world and I knew that he didn't want his old mother with an unbridled tongue queering his pitch. I was living at Tooting and I don't mind telling you I was very happy there.

"I had plenty of money, Norman saw to that—I will say he's always done the right thing by me—and I had a friend of whom I was very fond. He's dead now or I don't suppose I should be sitting here in a bed Queen Elizabeth did or didn't sleep in. I wouldn't have left him while he was alive."

"Did you come here after Cynthia . . . I mean Lady Mitcham . . . left?" Fleur asked.

"Not for a year or so. I think Norman was of the opinion that she might come back to him. He wouldn't divorce her at first, and then she insisted. There was scene after scene when she'd come down here and beg Norman to give her her freedom.

"He'd bought the house from her when they got married to give her an independent income of her own; but I believe what finally decided him was that she threatened to dispute his right to the estate—something to do with breaking entails, I believe.

"Anyway, he gave in eventually, and off she goes to Kenya with the man she wanted to marry; and then— would you believe it?—the very day the six months was up and Norman got his decree made absolute, the man was killed. A motor smash after a big cocktail party they had given to celebrate their wedding which was to have taken place the next day."

"How ghastly!" Fleur exclaimed. "What an awful thing to happen!"

"I've never seen Cynthia since," Mrs. Mitcham went on. "She changed her name by deed poll and went back to calling herself Lady Cynthia Ashwin—that's the Granton family name."

"But I'm sure I've seen her picture somewhere," Fleur said. "In the *Tatler* or one of the illustrated papers. She's very beautiful, isn't she?"

"Everybody says so," Mrs. Mitcham replied. "Never admired those thin, half-starved-looking women myself. She had charm and could make you think her very pleasant if she liked. She was certainly nice to me. I often think of the first time we met.

"Norman was afraid I would shock her. He was always a bit ashamed of me. But Cynthia laughed at all I said, capped some of my remarks, and when she was leaving bent and kissed me.

" 'We ought to have met before,' she says, 'I've been brought up to appreciate the genuine article—what I can't abide is pretence.'

"She looks at Norman under her eyelashes as she speaks and I guess that's a dig at him, but I was pleased

114

all the same. She's got an easy manner with her, you could tell she was a lady born and bred.

"She'd sit down and chat confidential-like, egging me on to express myself, while there was Norman dancing about like a cat on hot bricks, not knowing where to put his hands and feet and on tenterhooks in case I said something I oughtn't."

"I can't imagine Sir Norman like that," Fleur said. "He seems to me to be most self-composed."

"He is now," his mother agreed. "He's schooled himself to it. I'm always inclined to think that he's giving the perfect impersonation of the big businessman—you know the type you read about in magazines, cool and hard, ready to sign a cheque for a few hundred thousand without blinking an eyelid."

Fleur laughed.

"I think you are rather cruel about your son."

"Am I?" Mrs. Mitcham asked. "Perhaps I am. He doesn't seem to me to be a human being. I can't get past that high-chinned, stuck-up manner of his. I've always wanted the type of son who'd bound into the room, sit down on my bed and say: 'What do you think, Mum? I've just seduced the housemaid!' "

"You'd like nothing of the sort if it happened in reality," Fleur said severely.

She knew now that when Mrs. Mitcham talked like this she was talking for effect.

"Well, at least it would be a change from Norman, who lives the life of a monk and whose pleasures begin and end with the turning of a greasy wheel."

"What about the house?" Fleur asked softly. "He must still love that."

"I wonder," Mrs. Mitcham replied. "Sometimes I think he hates it."

When Fleur went down to dinner that evening she looked at Sir Norman with a new interest.

Strange to think that he had been through so much, that he had married and lost his wife, that he had loved the house in which he had worked as a boy and grown up to own it. She wished she knew more.

She had the feeling that all Mrs. Mitcham had told her had been to a certain extent hearsay.

She was certain with an intuitive certainty which needed no confirmation that Sir Norman had never discussed with anybody the intimate events of his life; what his mother had learnt she had pieced together laboriously from conversations with eyewitnesses and servants.

Fleur longed, as they sat at the large, silver-laden dining-table, to ask Sir Norman some intimate question about himself and to watch his reactions, but she was afraid.

Norman Mitcham inspired fear. Daily she was beginning to understand more clearly what Jack had meant when he had said "he's like a Juggernaut."

There was a relentlessness about him, one became more and more conscious of it with every new contact. Apart from that the man appeared to be dull; he had little or no small talk.

Fleur would often find the long silences at meals almost unbearable and she would chatter from nervousness rather than from having anything interesting to say.

She had tried to draw him out about the business and the work he was doing; but always he would put her off with a few conventional phrases, telling her nothing in detail, making no effort to respond to her tentative questions.

When she exclaimed over the treasures in the house he behaved in very much the same manner.

Occasionally he would give her dates or data about some particular picture; but he recited them rather as a lesson, a few sentences culled, as it were, from a guide-book—then he would lapse into silence again.

Tonight, looking at him as he sat opposite her, Fleur realised that he seldom glanced at her directly. It was as if he looked anywhere but into her eyes, deliberately avoiding taking in the details of her appearance.

And as they ate, indulging in desultory conversation with long intervals of silence between sentences, Fleur had a sudden idea.

"I believe he's afraid of me!" she thought.

And as the idea formulated itself in her mind she became almost certain that she had chanced on an important truth, perhaps the key to Norman Mitcham's whole character.

"He's afraid of women . . . all women. I wonder how much and why Cynthia made him suffer?"

CHAPTER TWELVE

Fleur walked slowly along the wide gallery leading to the west wing of the house.

Every now and then she stopped and inspected a chair or a picture frame for dust, conscientiously performing her duties of supervision, and yet she knew that this was a pretence.

She had another reason for moving about the house, one of which she was half-ashamed. It was curiosity—curiosity about the Priory's former owner and mistress, Norman Mitcham's wife.

Fleur's thoughts were continually on Lady Cynthia Ashwin—why, she could not tell.

She found herself thinking about her, wondering what she had been like, why she had married Norman Mitcham only to leave him and by her departure make herself an exile from her home and from all that was intimately connected with the history of her family.

For Fleur had learnt now that it was now not Sir Norman's good taste which she had admired the first day she had entered the Priory; the house had remained unchanged by his coming.

It was the Ashwins who had left a permanent memorial of themselves within the grey walls of a house which had been in their family for over five centuries.

It was impossible for Fleur not to think of Sir Norman and his mother as interlopers—at times she felt almost a personal resentment against them, especially Sir Norman.

When he was unusually morose and monosyllabic at meals she would fancy that the elegant Ashwins, looking down on them from their eminence on the panelled walls of the dining-room, sneered as if they asked—

"What can you expect from a mere manufacturer? We may have been bad, but we knew the arts and graces of life. This man only understands how to make wheels go round."

Fleur would chide herself for such thoughts; but Sir Norman was difficult and sometimes it was hard to hide her own boredom and longing, someone she could talk to, someone who would share her interests and relieve an almost overwhelming inner loneliness.

Gradually, as she absorbed the family history, she found herself becoming more and more curious about the last Ashwin to have lived here ... the Lady Cynthia.

Fleur became determined that somehow she would learn more about her, she found herself searching the house for some sign of her presence.

It was impossible for Cynthia, vivid and vivacious as Fleur imagined her, to have come and gone and left nothing behind.

Today Fleur was determined to go to inspect Cynthia's bedroom. She knew where it was. On her first tour of inspection Manvers, the head housemaid, who had taken her round, had passed a door in the west wing.

"What room is that?" Fleur had inquired.

"That room is kept closed," Manvers had replied. "Sir Norman's orders."

"Isn't it ever turned out?"

"Once a month and I do it myself."

Manvers was a gruff, uncommunicative sort of woman who resented Fleur's advent into the household and was determined to be as unhelpful as she dared.

Fleur said nothing at the time, she did not insist on

her right of going into the room, but now she meant to satisfy her curiosity. It was Manvers's day out, she was glad of that.

It was not that she was afraid of the elder woman, but that she was ashamed of the irrepressible impulse which sent her searching about the house for signs of Cynthia.

She reached the door of the room; a few steps further down the passage were the rooms used by Sir Norman. The room was locked, but the key was on the outside of the door. Fleur turned it. . . .

The first thing she noticed as she entered the room was a fragrance. It was very faint, almost imperceptible, yet it was there—a lovely, exotic and expensive scent.

"It was what I expected of her—she would smell like that," Fleur thought triumphantly.

She passed through the door and shut it behind her, then moved across the dimness of the room to raise a blind at the far end. The sunshine flooded in and she turned from the window.

Her first impression was one of disappointment. The room looked desolate. Somehow, ridiculously she told herself, she had expected it to seem more intimate, more reminiscent of the picture she had drawn for herself of Cynthia's character.

The bed was covered in peach satin, the carpet was of pale Nile-blue to match the walls. It was a lovely room. The Spanish furniture of carved wood had been painted silver, the dressing-table was a great slab of pink marble supported on a carved stand of silver.

There was an exquisite oil painting of the Italian school over the mantelpiece, flanked by glass mirrors which glittered and sparkled in the sunlight; a chandelier of Venetian glass hung from the ceiling.

This room told Fleur nothing, she knew no more than she had known when she had first come to the house. It was absurd to be so disappointed, yet somehow she had hoped to learn so much of this woman who had lived and suffered and run away.

Impulsively she opened a door at the far end. There was a bathroom decorated in pink and blue to match the bedroom. She shut the door again. Was there nothing else to be seen?

As she moved over the soft carpet she saw that one piece of the silvered furniture was a chest of drawers. Still half-accusingly she pulled open a drawer.

"It's my job," she thought, "to see that everything's tidy, the paper fresh."

And yet she knew she was following her own desires, not the instructions given her. The top drawer was empty, so was the next; but in the bottom drawer there was a collection of large, flat leather-bound books and a box.

Fleur's heart gave a leap, she knew at the first glance what they were. Photograph albums!

She opened them. Here was what she had hoped to find, snapshots of the Priory, of the gardens, groups of people standing with tennis racquets in their hands or sitting under the trees, obviously arrested in a moment of conversation to raise their heads and smile towards the photographer.

Fleur looked at each one, but amongst the many women portrayed she was not certain which was Cynthia. Perhaps she had been the photographer, perhaps she herself was not included in the groups.

Then, as she finished the first book and turned to the second, she found loose in the cover what she sought—a large photograph, taken from its frame. Here, at last, was Cynthia.

There was no doubt about that; it was easy to see the resemblance to many other Ashwin faces hanging in the galleries and on the stairs. The same broad forehead, the thin, well-bred nose and the heart-shaped face which Lawrence, Joshua Reynolds, Lely and Romney had admired and painted when they were at the height of their fame.

"I was not mistaken," Fleur thought, "she is lovely. No, more than lovely—beautiful."

She was dark, with her hair smooth and satiny as a raven's wing against her ears, and there was something proud and challenging in her large eyes and, in contradiction, something inviting in the curve of her lips.

From contemplation of the photograph Fleur turned avidly to the books again. Now she could recognise Cynthia again and again—in Switzerland, bathing at Monte Carlo, in the driving-seat of a racing-car, stepping into the cockpit of an aeroplane.

In all of them she was lovely, indeed exquisite, but individual, with a manner which had nothing in common with the glamour of film stars or the much advertised beauty of the average society woman.

Now Fleur remembered having seen her picture, in fact, she must have seen it many times, in illustrated papers. Cynthia was small, that was somehow surprising.

Fleur had expected her to be tall, slim and willowy; instead, in some of the groups she appeared quite tiny. And in all there were not many photographs.

Fleur put the last book down regretfully and looked again at the photograph. Yes, there was character in that face. Fleur put the photograph back where she had found it and got to her knees, ready to close the drawer.

Then she hesitated . . . put out her hand and opened a box; it was a square wooden box, unlocked. She lifted the lid to stare at what she saw inside.

There was a gold cigarette-case and a lighter to match, a pair of links with sapphire and diamond centres, thrown down carelessly as if their value was of no account, a leather wallet bearing the initials "N.M." and a tiny gold charm made in the shape of a car.

Fleur understood. These were the presents that Cynthia had given her husband.

Hastily she shut the lid, feeling now that she was prying, wishing that she had not intruded upon what was too intimate for the eyes of a stranger. But not before she saw one other thing, strange among such objects of value—a little doll of black china, dressed as a hula-hula girl.

It was tiny, the sort of thing one might buy at a fair or be given on a gala night at a restaurant. Why was that there too, Fleur wondered, and thought that perhaps Cynthia had given it to Norman as a mascot.

Had he ever been involved in such childish nonsense? It was almost impossible to imagine that he might have been, and yet when people were in love how very different they became.

She shut the drawer. It must have been Sir Norman who had brought these things in here to put them away where he could not see them—the photograph of Cynthia taken from its frame, the gifts she had given him.

"Yet how wrong, how utterly wrong," Fleur thought angrily, "to have left them where they could be seen by other people!"

Almost angrily she left the room, turning the key in the door. Although she had found what she had sought, she was not gratified; instead she was angry with Norman Mitcham and disliked him even more than she had before.

That was not the way to treat the memory of someone he had loved, she told herself—shutting up her room as if Cynthia were dead and throwing into a drawer for the servants to find the things which had once been mementoes of happy anniversaries and perhaps of happy hours together.

"Yet what can one expect?" she asked herself. "It is obvious the man has no finer feelings. I'm not surprised that Cynthia left him. He must have hurt her, must have outraged everything she treasured and thought sacred."

It was time for Mrs. Mitcham to be awakened from her afternoon rest. As Fleur reached her room, her lady's maid was just coming out of it; the blinds were drawn up and Mrs. Mitcham was propped up again against her pillows.

"Come in, dear. What have you been doing?"

Fleur told the truth.

"I've been going round the house."

"Did you find anything?"

Fleur started.

"What do you mean?" she stammered.

"Nothing in particular," Mrs. Mitcham replied, "but when people go looking round, they generally hope to find something interesting."

"There's always something new to learn here," Fleur said, feeling calmer and less startled.

"Only about them as is dead and gone," Mrs. Mitcham said. "I like living people myself. Barham tells me we are likely to have some soldiers in the park for the next few days—they are going to have manoeuvres round here. Better look them over and see if you can't find yourself a new young man."

"I don't want a young man," Fleur replied. "You ought to know that by this time."

"Nonsense! Every woman wants a man. You can't kid me with that business of being happier alone. You'd better get yourself a husband, and get him quick; and if you can't get a husband, find a lover. There's plenty of them about, from all accounts."

Fleur moved restlessly.

"I've told you," she said, "that I'm not interested in that sort of thing. I like working for you and I hope I give satisfaction."

"Hoity-toity!" Mrs. Mitcham retorted. "Now you're offended. You're a funny girl, I can't always guess at what you're thinking. Not that that doesn't make you more interesting. But whatever you say, you put on one of your prettiest dresses and hope that some of their soldier lads will pop in for a cup of tea."

There was no sign of any troops arriving before dinner and Fleur thought that Barham must for once have been mistaken.

Then, just as she and Sir Norman were finishing their meal, the door of the dining-room opened and Barham announced—"Captain Anthony Ashwin."

Fleur looked up and saw a tall, good-looking young man come into the room.

"Hello, Norman," the newcomer said in a cheery voice. "I've come to beg the hospitality of your park. It's a bit of a coincidence their sending me here, isn't it? When they told me where I was going I could hardly believe it."

He shook hands with Sir Norman who, Fleur noticed, seemed none too pleased to see him, and then stared across the table at her until, somewhat ungraciously, the introduction was effected. Anthony Ashwin sat down in the chair Barham held for him.

Barham told him that he could get something in a few minutes.

"Anything will do; and tell old Mother Johnson that I'm as hungry as a hunter. She's still here, I suppose?"

He asked the question of Norman, who replied curtly:

"Yes, Mrs. Johnson is still with us."

"The best cook in England," Anthony Ashwin said enthusiastically. "Don't you think so?"

He spoke directly to Fleur.

"She's marvellous," Fleur agreed, "especially as it's wartime."

"Well, Norman ought to be able to get all he wants," Captain Ashwin replied. "Do you mean to say you haven't got a finger in the black market, Norman! Why, with your influence and bank account it ought to be easy."

"Perhaps I'm too patriotic," Norman Mitcham suggested quietly.

"Well, don't be too patriotic to offer me a really decent drink," Anthony Ashwin laughed. "The whole way here—and it's been a hell of a day, I can tell you—I've been thinking of having a glass of Croft '08. Don't tell me you've drunk it all!"

"No, there's plenty left, I imagine."

"Well then, let's drink and be merry."

Captain Ashwin had, Fleur thought, naturally high spirits which made everything he said sound gay. He

125

was a very vivid contrast to his host, sitting morosely silent and—Fleur thought—inclined to be resentful at the intrusion.

She herself found it difficult not to respond to the laughter and gaiety in Captain Ashwin's blue eyes.

Thankfully she remembered that she had taken Mrs. Mitcham's advice and had put on one of her prettiest dresses that evening. It had come amongst her other clothes, which, she discovered, had been deposited at the bank by Sylvia and which had been forwarded to the Priory on the day before.

"How's the factory, Norman?" Anthony Ashwin was asking.

"It's making quite an adequate contribution to the war effort, I think," Norman Mitcham replied.

"I bet it is if you've got anything to do with it. They ought to make you Minister of Supply and then we'd get going."

"I think I'm more likely to be of use where I am," Sir Norman said with a faint smile.

"Have you been round the factory yet?" Captain Ashwin asked Fleur.

"No, I haven't," she replied, and then, greatly daring, she added: "I haven't been asked."

"Norman, how ungracious of you!" Captain Ashwin exclaimed. "Here's a lovely lady dying to be impressed by your ability and you don't even want to show off. The trouble with you, old man, is that you don't know how to make the best of yourself.

"Now, if I were owner of the Mitcham works, I should have a statue of myself at every entrance and a large one on the sports ground. People would be allowed to come and worship before it and flowers would be received every third Thursday."

Fleur laughed. Sir Norman, she noticed, seemed unamused.

Barham came back with the food and Captain Ashwin started to tuck into it as if he had not eaten a good meal for days.

"By Jove! Norman," he exclaimed, "cream and butter! I didn't know such things still existed.

"We still have our farm."

"Yes, of course. And how is old Doughty and that pretty daughter of his? What's her name—Dolly, who used to look after the dairy? I remember trying to kiss her once when she was milking and the cow kicked me."

Interesting though Captain Ashwin's conversation was, Fleur felt she must attend to her duties. Although she dined with Sir Norman, she always took coffee upstairs with his mother and she knew that the old lady would be waiting.

"Will you excuse me?" she said, getting to her feet. "I think I must go upstairs to Mrs. Mitcham."

"Oh, is she still here?" Anthony Ashwin asked. "Give her my love. I'll come up and see her later. But must you leave us?"

"Miss Garton is here as companion to my mother," Sir Norman remarked coldly.

"Well, if you must go," Anthony Ashwin said, getting to his feet; "but I shall be seeing you later."

Fleur sensed rather than felt Sir Norman's disapproval as she went through the door held open for her by Captain Ashwin. He smiled at her as she went by, and before the door was shut and she was out of hearing, she heard him say:

"By Jove! That's a good-looker! Where did you pick her up, Norman?"

She ran upstairs with flaming cheeks to find the old lady looking like a cat who's been at the cream.

"What did I tell you?" she asked. "And you needn't have hurried. I knew you wouldn't be wanting to come upstairs to me while there was interesting company in the dining-room."

"He sent you his love," Fleur said breathlessly, "and he wants to come and see you."

"And so he shall," Mrs. Mitcham approved, "and Norman shan't prevent him if I can help it. I always liked that boy—I suppose because he's a bad lot. Most

127

of the Ashwins are bad, but he's the worst of them all."

"In what way?"

"Oh, the usual way—cards and women—but he was always Cynthia's favourite cousin."

"A first cousin?"

"Yes, that's right and they were brought up together as children. I often wonder if she didn't have rather a soft spot for him in her heart. Anyway, I believe he was always here when she first married Norman, and after she'd gone off Anthony did a lot of the negotiating between the two of them.

"I expect Norman hates him, but then, there's few people Norman doesn't hate one way or another. It certainly doesn't worry me what his likes and dislikes are. You go downstairs and tell young Anthony that I want to see him."

"He hasn't finished his dinner yet."

"Oh, well, there's plenty of time. I hear that he's billeting his men in the barns down behind the garage. Best place he could put them, but then, of course, he'd know that."

"He certainly seems to know how to make himself at home," Fleur said. "He said the one thing he'd been looking forward to all the way here was a glass of port."

"And Anthony wouldn't stop at a glass either if I know him. I want to see him—it'll be a breath of life to have a look at that cocky young fellow-me-lad. Here, ring the bell for me."

Fleur did as she was told and it was answered by the lady's maid.

"Evans, go downstairs and tell Barham that I want the gentlemen to have their port up here," Mrs. Mitcham said. "And tell him too that I won't take no for an answer."

"Very good, madam."

Evans sniffed, and Fleur knew that she did not approve of such dissipation for the old lady. She adored Mrs. Mitcham in her own way, being jealous and resentful if anyone else did anything for her.

She had been prepared for Fleur to be a natural enemy, but gradually, when she found that Fleur was not
going to interfere with anything that concerned her employer's health, Evans was coming round to being con-
descendingly affable.

"And, Evans," Mrs. Mitcham screeched as the maid
was leaving the room, "give me my powder-puff and my
jewel-case. I'd better posh myself up a bit. Not that Anthony Ashwin's likely to look at me when you're about,
my dear."

"I can't believe that he's the sort of young man that
you approve of," Fleur said. "After all you've told me I
think the best thing for me to do is to go to bed right
away."

"When I was talking to you earlier this evening,"
Mrs. Mitcham retorted, "I told you to get yourself a
husband or a lover. Anthony would be an impossible
husband, but a good lover, if I'm any judge."

Evans snorted her disapproval as she put the jewel-
case down on the bed. Mrs. Mitcham waited until she
had gone out of the room, shutting the door sharply behind her.

"Poor old Evans, she was crossed in love many years
ago. She can't bear anyone else should have any fun.
It's good for her to be teased, but somehow it seems
unfair that some women should have men round them
like flies round a honeypot and others, like Evans, have
one chance and lose it. Oh well, no one can say that I
missed my opportunities."

She opened the jewel-case, clasped a string of pearls
round her neck, added a few more rings to the fine collection already glittering on her swollen fingers and put
on her diamond bracelet.

"Look at that ring—see it sparkle," Mrs. Mitcham
gloated. "I love jewels, can't have too many of them.
When I came here to live Norman said to me:

" 'Mother, you can have anything in the world you
want. Now what would you like?'

" 'Diamonds,' I replied, 'and plenty of them.' I haven't

earned much either by virtue or sin in my life—in fact I don't mind telling you I've given away a good deal more than I've got—and so in my old age I might as well have the satisfaction of decking myself out like I always wanted to when I was young.

"Poor Norman, he can't understand, of course, but he does his best. He gave me some jewellery then and another bit every Christmas and every birthday. If I live till I'm ninety I'll have quite a decent collection to leave to whom I choose."

"It ought to go to your grandchildren," Fleur said.

"That's what I tell Norman," his mother replied, "but he looks as much like providing me with any as Evans does of having triplets. Oh, well, I guess I'll find a home for them where they'll be appreciated."

She glanced at Fleur as she spoke and the latter had the impression that she was not the first companion who had been tempted with hints of benefiting when the old lady died.

Somehow the thought of those women lusting over the jewels, yearning to possess them, made Fleur feel faintly sick.

"I should be buried with them if I were you," she suggested tartly, and knew that for once she had the last word.

She put the jewel-case back in the drawer. Mrs. Mitcham had only just finished powdering her nose and was glancing in a hand-glass to see if her wig was on straight when the door opened.

It was Sir Norman.

"Where's Anthony?" his mother demanded.

"I've sent him off to see to his men," Norman replied brusquely. "It's too late for you to be receiving visitors."

CHAPTER THIRTEEN

Fleur walked into her own little sitting-room and sank down wearily into one of the armchairs.

It was only ten o'clock and she was not sleepy; at the same time she felt exhausted with the scene which had just taken place—Mrs. Mitcham screeching abuse at her son; Sir Norman calm, imperturbable and obstinately determined.

And herself striving to keep aloof and indifferent, but being dragged willy-nilly into the argument by Mrs. Mitcham.

It was Evans who had brought the episode to a welcome conclusion. She had shooed both Sir Norman and Fleur out of the bedroom, clucking at them in a furious undertone like a hen who thinks her chick is in danger.

"You know it's bad for the heart ... she can't stand this sort of thing ... I can't think what you're thinking of ..."

Sir Norman and Fleur found themselves outside in the passage with the door closed sharply behind them—Evans's invariable way of expressing disapproval.

Fleur felt embarrassed, and for a moment she thought that Sir Norman was slightly nonplussed; then he said gravely, as if anxious for once to give an explanation and to excuse himself:

"Any excitement is bad for her, but especially late at night."

"I should imagine that there are degrees of excitement," Fleur replied coldly, "some bad and some not so bad."

"By which you mean?" Sir Norman started accusingly, then checked the words abruptly.

For a moment Fleur had fancied that he was about to argue with her, to be human for once. But instead, as if he metaphorically shrugged his shoulders and dismissed her opinion as one of supreme indifference, he drew himself up and said in his most forbidding voice:

"Where my mother's health is concerned I follow out the doctor's orders conscientiously and I hope you, Miss Garton, will try to do the same."

With that he turned and walked away down the passage. Fleur had a wild desire to shout after him, to finish all she would like to say, and then she remembered that such vulgarity had no power to stir him.

His mother, screeching and belabouring him with her tongue, had made no impression on his imperturbability. It was all rather undignified and somewhat sordid, Fleur thought.

At such times it was easy to see that Mrs. Mitcham told the truth when she spoke of her own common origin. The expressions she used when she was angry were the type that the average woman of any class would be likely to hear only in a bar or among men of the rougher sort.

Wearily Fleur pushed back the hair from her forehead and closed her eyes. The true atmosphere of the house, its silence and peace, began once more to encompass her.

It was only in Mrs. Mitcham's room that such calm was lost, and even then Fleur had the feeling that the noise and vitality she expended was very transitory, a mere ripple on the surface beneath which the waters of antiquity were still and deep.

A sudden scuffling noise made her open her eyes and listen.

She wondered what it was; it was repeated and she

132

realised it came from the tiny porch outside her window. Hardly large enough to be called a balcony, it was the roof of an ancient stone doorway which led into the garden.

The noise came again and then, so suddenly that her heart leapt with the shock, there came a tap on her window.

"Who is it?" she asked, aware that her voice was several tones too high.

In answer the heavy curtains were moved aside and the head and shoulders of a man appeared through them.

"Did I startle you?" Anthony Ashwin asked.

"What are you doing?" Fleur asked, "How could you ...? I mean ... how did you get here?"

He laughed at her surprise and came into the room, closing the curtains behind him to prevent the light from showing into the garden.

"Enter villain by trapdoor," he said jokingly, then added: "I'm sorry if I frightened you, but I couldn't resist doing once again what I've done a hundred times. This used to be my favourite way into the house in the old days.

"You see, my uncle was of the old school—everyone had to be in by ten o'clock, the whole place bolted and barred—you know the type. But 'stone walls do not a prison make'—not to yours truly anyway, so Cynthia and I always used what we called the side door for our nocturnal adventures."

"But isn't it terribly dangerous?" Fleur asked.

"Not a bit," Anthony Ashwin replied. "Besides, if you are very good and promise to tell nobody, I'll show you the secret tomorrow. There are projecting iron rungs put into the porch to form a nice easy ladder. It cost me a month's allowance to get one of the estate carpenters to do it for us."

"All the same," Fleur said, collecting herself, "you oughtn't to come here like this. Sir Norman said you'd gone to see about your men."

"I've seen about them all right," Anthony replied, "and they don't want me fussing round. Besides, the night's still young and I thought I'd like a little feminine companionship. That's where you come in, but, remembering my Omar Khayyam, there's something besides 'thou'."

Fleur had to smile.

"I suppose you mean a jug of wine."

"Exactly!" Captain Ashwin said with approval. "I see you're intelligent as well as beautiful."

It was difficult to be severe with such impertinence. Fleur giggled despite a resolution to be unbending.

"If you'll excuse me," he went on, "I'll pop down and tell Barham that I want the rest of that port. Norman hustled me so, I only had a couple of glasses before I found myself outside the front door."

"Barham will be horrified!"

"Don't you believe it. Barham has the Ashwin interests at heart. He's got me out of many scrapes as a boy and I wouldn't be surprised if he was ready to help me into one now."

His eyes were twinkling and as he reached the door, he stopped and smiled at her invitingly.

"Don't go away, beautiful," he pleaded. "If you are not here when I return, I shall knock on every door in the house until I find you."

When he was gone Fleur stood for a moment, both hands against her cheeks.

"This is wrong!" she thought. "If Sir Norman hears of this I shall doubtless get the sack!"

Yet she knew that she was not going to protect overmuch. It was fun to talk to anyone so gay and lighthearted as Anthony Ashwin; it was amusing in this house of age and antiquity to find a young man clambering in through the window, prepared to enleague her with his own adventurous spirit.

Oh, well, what did it matter? The worst Sir Norman could do would be to send her packing, and after all, who was she—a mere employee in the house—to with-hold hospitality from an Ashwin?

Anthony returned a few minutes later and, following behind him, carrying a silver tray on which there were a decanter of port and two glasses, came Barham.

He set the wine down on the small table near the sofa, and asked:

"Is there anything else you'd like, sir?"

"Not that I can think of at the moment," Anthony Ashwin replied, "unless ... yes, unless it's one of those really good cigars—the ones you used to keep specially for me."

"We have one box left," Barham said with pride. "They're not obtainable now."

"Well, open it, you old miser."

"Very good, sir."

Barham left the room with a slight smirk on his lips. It was the first time Fleur had seen him look pleased since she had been in the house. Usually his air was one of pompous melancholy, as if he was eternally regretting the times were not what they were.

"You shock me," Fleur said later, as Anthony, sitting back on the sofa, sipped his port, an open box of cigars beside him.

"That's the most flattering thing that's been said to me for a long time," Anthony replied. "I've always believed that it was impossible to say or do anything nowadays which was original enough to surprise the modern young woman, let alone shock her."

"You know what I mean," Fleur said severely. "Being here like this, opening Sir Norman's last box of really good cigars. You heard what Barham said—that it was impossible to get any more."

"Good gracious me, Midas won't know the difference between these and the tenpenny sort you buy outside the works."

"What did you call him?"

"Midas. We always called him that in the old days."

135

"Because he is so rich?"

"No, because he has ass's ears. You remember the chap in the fairy story who was always trying to conceal from the world his deformity. Well, that's poor old Norman—always trying to hide his somewhat unsavoury origin."

"You mean he's a snob?" Fleur asked.

"Not exactly," Anthony answered, taking another sip of port. "That doesn't describe him well. No, Norman was always pretending—I don't know whether he does it now, he certainly did in the old days—acting, if you like to put it that way, and doing it damned badly.

"Here am I—the 'Squire of the manor', 'the country gentleman at home', and all that sort of thing. My goodness! There's many a time I've laughed myself silly seeing Norman in Uncle Walter's place, fancying himself as 'Lord Mitcham of Greystone Priory'. It made me laugh, but I always thought Cynthia felt rather sick."

"That doesn't seem a bit in keeping with his character as I've seen it."

"How do you get on with him?"

"I don't—that's just the point," Fleur admitted. "I think he's the most difficult person to talk to I've ever met in my life."

"That's what we used to find. Lord! The way that man was able to cast a blight on a party. We'd all be here, the old gang, Cynthia like a star in the midst of us, and then Norman would come home. You'd feel the atmosphere drop about ten degrees. No wonder Cynnie couldn't stick it."

"Is she happy now?" Fleur asked. "Mrs. Mitcham told me about the tragedy before she was married."

"Happy! Haven't you heard? No, I suppose they wouldn't tell you, but she's ill—desperately ill."

"I'm sorry," Fleur said quickly, and genuinely meant it.

"Consumption, of course; all we Ashwins have a tendency that way, but Cynnie always seemed so strong. Still, it's got her and she's in a sanatorium not far from here—near Melchester. It's the best in the country. She was in Switzerland until the war started and then, luckily, her doctor got the wind up and insisted on her being sent home by air."

"Poor thing!" Fleur said.

It was absurd, and yet she felt as if she were grieving over a personal friend. Cynthia Ashwin, whom she had always imagined so gay, so happy, to be suffering from that fell and dreaded disease, coughing her heart out, knowing that it was in the family, that there was little chance of her recovery.

"Does Sir Norman know this?" she asked.

Anthony Ashwin shrugged his shoulders.

"I expect so. I haven't seen the old boy for a long time. I don't think he cares for me much, as you may have guessed from the enthusiastic way he greeted me this evening. Heavens! How this place has changed. In the past there was welcome on the map for everyone, no one would think of passing the gates without dropping in.

"From the time Cynnie was old enough to play hostess—and that was when she was pretty young—the place was always packed with people. My mother died when I was quite small and I lived here except for short intervals with my father. I loved the place, it was my real home.

"I hated the idea of Cynthia handing it over. Ridiculous really, because I suppose all this sort of thing is finished, or will be by the time the war is over; what with income tax and E.P.T., I don't suppose even millionaires like Norman will be able to carry on."

"What an awful idea!" Fleur exclaimed. "I love this house, too. That sounds presumptuous because I have only been here a short time, and yet I never imagined anything could be so beautiful, so exquisite in every detail."

"Nevertheless, it belongs to the past," Anthony Ashwin insisted. "So many things do. Let's talk about the present—let's talk about you. Tell me about yourself."

137

Fleur knew that he deliberately changed the conversation, as if the reminiscence was painful to him; but, whatever the reason, it was swept away in the ardour with which he attempted to flirt with her, using every experienced wile of an art in which he appeared to be an adept.

She was amused, even while she told herself that she was too disillusioned to be interested in a man again. But it was with a feeling of guilt that she heard the clock on the mantelpiece strike twelve. She jumped to her feet.

"Midnight! I'd no idea it was so late. You must go."

"With daylight-saving it's really only ten o'clock," Anthony argued, "so I can stay a little longer and still not outrage the proprieties."

"Nonsense!" Fleur said. "You must go at once."

"Must I?" He walked across the room deliberately and put his arms round her. "This has been an oasis of delight in a desert of deadly dull military duties. We're in a world of enchantment all our own, Fleur. How I love that name—it suits you. Don't send me away."

"You must be crazy," Fleur said, struggling. "Go away at once or I shall be really angry."

"You won't. I'm not afraid of that. But if you insist, I'll be good—for tonight, at any rate."

With a gentle kiss upon her cheek he let her go and turned towards the window.

"Good night, beautiful. Dream of me."

"I shall do nothing of the sort," Fleur replied; and then he was gone, as swiftly and incredibly as he had come.

Fleur looked round the room, feeling she must have imagined the whole episode, but the empty decanter was proof enough, the grey ash and the stubbed-out end of the cigar.

She hesitated, not knowing whether to tidy up, to pack away the evidences of the crime for fear of the housemaids finding it in the morning, or leave it to Barham's discretion. She chose the latter course and went to bed.

Men are all the same, she thought dispassionately. A pretty face and they are all over the place until a prettier one comes along! Oh, well, I can play that game too—laugh and be merry; but I'll never, never let myself love anyone again!

Despite every resolution her thoughts turned to Jack and she felt the cruel stabbing pain such memories always involved.

"I will forget him," she cried aloud defiantly in the darkness. "I'll make other men suffer as I am suffering; I will become hard and indifferent."

Her voice broke on a sob.

"Oh, Jack! Jack!" she whispered into her pillow.

In the morning she reproached herself for being weak with Anthony Ashwin, but half-heartedly, as one might conventionally rebuke an amusing child.

"What does it matter?" she asked herself, seeing the dark lines under her eyes, lines which told their own story of a sleepless night.

"I shan't let it happen again," she added but knew, even as the words formulated themselves, that she was glad that there was a chance of Anthony and his men staying for some days. Perhaps Anthony could help her to forget.

It was Saturday and Sir Norman was in to luncheon, Fleur half-hoped that Anthony would appear, but there was no sign of him and they sat down in silence while Barham handed round the big silver dishes. When they were alone, Sir Norman cleared his throat.

"I feel," he said, "that I owe you an apology for last night, Miss Garton. Thinking it over afterwards, I realised I was wrong. My mother is old and I know that she shouldn't get over-excited, but perhaps at that age happiness is preferable to anything, even if it must be purchased at the expense of health."

Fleur was surprised, so surprised that for a moment

she had no answer ready. She had spent the morning listening to Mrs. Mitcham's abuse of her son; the old lady had slept badly and felt ill.

She was querulous and irritable, venting her spite on all who approached her, including Evans who, however, was used to it and received all remarks addressed to her with nothing more provocative than a disdainful sniff.

For a moment Sir Norman's apology made Fleur feel ashamed. She was not sure why except that it showed a generosity with which she had not previously credited him.

She remembered how Anthony had laughed at him last night. Awkwardly she tried to respond.

"I shouldn't worry too much, Sir Norman," she said. "I think, as a matter of fact, your mother is far stronger than you imagine and she does love seeing people. I don't believe they tire her half as much as the doctors make out.

"Don't you think in the medical profession that it's often a stock prescription to order 'rest and quiet'? Rather like telling you to give up smoking and cocktails whether one indulges in them or not."

"Sometimes I feel I was wrong to bring her down here," Sir Norman said in a quiet voice as if he was speaking half to himself rather than to Fleur. "She loved London—the pavements were the breath of life to her. People would run in and out; she could gossip with them and not be so conscious of being bedridden."

"I don't think you'd like her to be there now with the likelihood of raids," Fleur said. "But in peace-time I should imagine that she would have been happier in a town."

"Then you don't think she's happy?" Sir Norman asked sharply.

"I didn't mean to put it quite like that," Fleur said quickly. "I think your mother has a tremendous capacity for making the best of things, for finding amusement and entertainment wherever she may be. I only said that perhaps, under different circumstances, London might have made her still happier."

She offered the lame explanation quickly, anxious to erase the impression made by her unconsidered words; then, as she finished, she realised that Sir Norman was disappointed.

There was no doubt about it, there was an expression on his face which was almost wistful, as if he knew he personally had failed. For a moment Fleur could hardly believe it and then she thought—

"So he does care for his mother ... does love her and wants to do what is best for her."

Then, as if a shutter was released, he reverted to his usual inscrutable expression and to silence.

Fleur was in the garden when Anthony Ashwin came striding across the lawn towards her. She was glad to see him and was honest enough to admit it as she watched him come, bareheaded, a cigar between his lips.

Mrs. Mitcham was asleep and Fleur had taken the opportunity to go into the garden, walking through the rose garden on to the green sward which led to the Grecian temple.

"Barham told me I should find you here," Anthony said, holding her hand longer than was necessary.

Fleur wondered if he had gone to Barham primarily to find out her whereabouts or to get himself another of Sir Norman's priceless cigars.

She found it hard to meet Anthony's eyes as, bold and inviting, they looked down into hers. She looked away from him, shy, yet conscious of a warm glow.

It was nice to know one was attractive, to read the obvious compliments as yet unsaid in a man's eyes; it was like the coming of spring again after a long, hard winter of misery and discontent.

"Mrs. Mitcham is asleep," she said primly. "When she wakes at four o'clock, I do hope you will go and see her. She is looking forward to it so much."

"Yes, I'll go and see the old girl if it gives her any pleasure," Anthony answered; "but to be truthful, I like women to be young and blooming as a rose. That's what you look like in that pink dress."

"Thank you, sir," Fleur mockingly dropped him a curtsy.

He slipped his arm through hers and drew her along with him.

"Come and look at the temple. It's full of ghosts—I want you to help me lay them."

"What sort of ghosts?" Fleur asked, embarrassed at his touch, but not certain how to make the effort to release herself.

"Fair ones, dark ones—I think one was red-headed," he teased.

"So many?"

"I was always brought up to believe in safety in numbers. Weren't you?"

"Certainly not. No nice girl is. One sits at home smugly waiting until Mr. Right drops down the chimney."

"But what if Mr. Wrong comes sneaking in through the bathroom window?"

"That's where the trouble begins," Fleur replied and they both laughed.

The sun was shining and they were young. Why shouldn't she escape from her own black thoughts and bitter memories, Fleur wondered.

Yet when they reached the privacy of the little temple and Anthony, holding out his arms, told her his ideas of laying the ghosts of the past, she felt a strange reluctance to continue the flirtation.

Although it was impossible not to like Anthony Ashwin, she was beginning to see where the charming veneer wore thin—little things, but nevertheless revealing even in their mere triviality.

For instance, he had chucked the half-smoked cigar away before he entered the temple. It was with difficulty she caught back the words of reproach. It was waste, and it was not his to waste.

And again, the way he sneered, slightly but perceptibly, at Sir Norman—"Let's hope Midas is not susceptible to Greek architecture this afternoon."

"Why can't they let the man alone?" Fleur thought.

First, Mrs. Mitcham, now Anthony Ashwin, both benefiting one way or another from Sir Norman and yet apparently without a good word to say for him. It was wrong, it was definitely, in schoolboy parlance, "not cricket".

Yet with Anthony's eyes looking into hers she found it difficult not to reciprocate, not to let herself drift the way this charming reprobate wished.

It was not love, of course; it was no more than the pleasure of receiving a bouquet of lovely flowers or a bottle of expensive perfume, little enough in themselves yet bringing one a feeling of gladness and delight.

"You are quite lovely," Anthony told her as they stood there, her head turned away from him because his lips were close. "If you were alone in the house with any other man save Norman I should suspect the worst. As it is, I shall do my best to make up for his deficiencies and come knocking on your door this evening."

There was no mistaking what he meant and uneasily, Fleur moved away to walk to the little stone window.

"You're making a mistake," she said, in a voice which tried to be cool. "I'm not that sort of a girl."

"You're adorable," Anthony replied, "and that's enough recommendation for anyone."

"You're incorrigible," Fleur flashed at him, and turning round, added quite firmly: "If I must put it plainly to you, the answer is 'no'—but thank you all the same."

"You can't mean that."

"But I do."

"What are you keeping yourself for?" Anthony demanded. "Your old age? Haven't you read what's written on the sundial in the rose garden—'Gather ye rosebuds while ye may'?"

143

"Do you consider yourself a rosebud?"

"No, but you are," he replied.

Taking her in his arms despite her resistance, he kissed her masterfully and passionately.

"Please ... please ..." she begged.

But Anthony laughed at her, his lips seeking hers. Again he kissed her and again, his passion holding her, demanding, wordlessly, but fiercely, her surrender.

"No! No! No!" Determined, she pushed him away from her. "I hate you! I hate all men!"

"I'll teach you to love me, Fleur ... let me teach you."

"Leave me alone; I'm angry—really angry, but it's my own fault—I shouldn't have come here with you."

"You've laid those ghosts ... I'm very grateful." Anthony spoke with mock humility. Despite her desire to remain angry, Fleur felt her mouth twitch at the corners.

"I must go back to the house," she said severely, clutching at her escaping dignity. "It must be after four o'clock."

"It's half-past," Anthony said triumphantly, looking at his wrist-watch. Fleur gave a little cry.

"I knew you'd get me into trouble before you'd finished."

"My goodness! That's a nice thing to say to a man when you've done nothing but say no," Anthony retorted.

She laughed, as she hurried through the temple door into the garden.

Then the words in which she had framed a reply died on her lips, for approaching the temple and within earshot was Sir Norman Mitcham.

CHAPTER FOURTEEN

Once, soon after Arthur Garton had married Sylvia, Fleur had come home unexpectedly early one evening from a dinner party and found her stepmother in the drawing-room with a young man.

As she opened the door, there had been a scuffle and they had started apart from each other, obviously having been interrupted in the midst of a close and intimate embrace.

Fleur had found it difficult to forget the startled, guilty expression on their faces, the uneasy, unnatural atmosphere of embarrassment and her own feeling of disgust.

That moment came back to her now as Sir Norman drew nearer, and she felt ashamed.

She tried to assume an air of nonchalance, to bolster herself up with an inner defiance; but she knew that she had fallen short of her own standards and was humiliated.

"I was looking for you, Miss Garton," Sir Norman said, and she fancied that there was an unusually strong note of disapproval in his tones. "My mother is awake and needs you."

"I am going to her now. I had no idea that it was so late."

"You must blame me for that, Norman," Anthony Ashwin interposed.

Sir Norman looked at him and answered quietly: "I had every intention of doing so."

There was a tension between the two men too obvious to be misunderstood. Hastily Fleur turned towards the house.

"You will excuse me," she said, "if I hurry on," and was gone before they could reply.

As she ran across the garden, she felt near to tears.

"Why am I such a fool?" she asked herself. "Why did I let myself get involved in all this? I hate Anthony Ashwin! I hate all men!"

She hurried up the wide staircase, then stopped for a moment outside Mrs. Mitcham's door while she ran her hands hastily over her dishevelled hair and tried to control her quickened breathing. Then she knocked.

There was no answer and she knocked again. The door opened abruptly and Evans stood there with her finger on her lips.

Before Fleur could speak she came out through the door, shutting it very, very gently behind her.

"Don't make a noise," Evans said reprovingly. "She's not awake yet. It will do her good to have a long rest after that bad night—and I'm not saying who's to blame for that, either."

"But I don't understand. I thought . . ."

The words died away. So Mrs. Mitcham had not required her. Sir Norman had come in search of her and told a deliberate lie. Why?

She asked the question again and again in the privacy of her own room. What, she wondered, could have been Sir Norman's motive? Dislike of Anthony?

Surely he would not let such a feeling influence him to the extent of telling a falsehood to one of his employees—a lie which was bound to be discovered?

"I don't understand it," Fleur thought.

She walked restlessly up and down. She felt that Anthony's coming had involved her in a chain of intrigue from which it would be wiser once and for all to escape.

Barham knowing that he had come to her sitting-room. Sir Norman discovering them alone in the temple . . . it was all unpleasant, it made her feel undignified and rather degraded.

"I shall leave," Fleur told herself.

Yet she knew that above all things she would hate to leave the Priory. She had not been pretending when she had told Anthony that she loved it.

In a month or so I shall be strong enough to do war work, she thought, then I shall have to leave anyway.

And yet she knew that Sir Norman could doubtless get her exempted and wondered if he would take the trouble.

Perhaps he was already considering dispensing with her services, perhaps that was why he had deliberately sent her in from the garden, determined that her behaviour should not set a bad example to the household.

And what had he said to Anthony after she had left.

It was like a nightmare, these questions coming one upon another, haunting her, giving her no peace from their insistence. Fleur was thankful when Mrs. Mitcham was awake and Evans came to fetch her. Anything was better than being alone with her thoughts, alone with the restlessness of her own mind.

She gave the old lady her tea, read to her, and then at last it was time for dinner. As Fleur changed, she knew that she was dreading the moment when she would see Sir Norman again.

She half-played with the idea of sending down a message to say she had a headache; but then, determined not to be cowardly, she forced herself to go downstairs, her head held high.

"If only Anthony Ashwin was going to be there," she thought.

Anything was better than one of those long, dreary meals with their awkward silences, and now the added trial of wondering what Sir Norman was thinking about her.

To Fleur's surprise, however, the meal started well. Sir Norman began almost at once to talk about an in-

147

spection which was to be held at the works the following day. The Minister of Aircraft Production was to be present and was to come back to the house later for a meal before proceeding to London.

There were various arrangements to be made; they discussed them, and then Sir Norman went on to speak of how the factory had expanded since the Minister's last visit.

"In only a few months we have doubled our output," he said. "That's something, at any rate; and at this rate of progress our returns by next year should be greater than anything the Germans can achieve in a single one of their factories."

He spoke enthusiastically and Fleur saw for the first time how close to his heart was the business he himself had created.

"What made you think of starting a motor works?" she asked.

Sir Norman looked at her with a faint smile.

"Are you really interested?"

"But of course," Fleur replied, and with a sudden flash of independence she added: "I shouldn't ask you if I wasn't."

"I believe that's true," Sir Norman said unexpectedly, and then he started to talk.

He told Fleur how, as a boy, he had always wanted to own a bicycle. There was something in the idea of propelling oneself along which fascinated him; and from attaining one ambition he went on to yearn for a car.

Through sheer hard work he became a qualified mechanic and then a partner in a firm of repairers. There were three of them in the business, all about the same age, and they worked eighteen hours a day to keep their heads above water.

It was in the days when motor cars were in their infancy and they thought out various improvements on the cars which were brought in for repair and finally evolved the tremendous idea of building a model of their own.

They worked night and day on this car, and when it was completed they realised they had something good, something which was not on the market.

The question then was, of course, the finding of capital, but by one of those lucky coincidences which do happen in real life, they sold their original car to an eccentric, exceedingly wealthy old man who took a fancy to the three young men.

He financed them and they started the Mitcham Motor works. The business was put in Norman's name because he was the eldest, and then, when things were really beginning to get going, the war broke out in 1914 and they all enlisted.

Norman was wounded very soon after he arrived in France and was invalided home again. He was in hospital with a badly damaged foot for nearly six months before he was discharged from the Army.

He kept the works going, but first one partner was killed, then the other. In 1918 he was the sole owner, for the "three musketeers" as they might have called themselves, had left their shares to each other.

Sir Norman told the story badly, stating his facts baldly and without theatrical effect, yet even so he could not destroy the drama of it.

Fleur could fill in so much of what was left unsaid; but once Sir Norman reached the start of his great success after the war, he lapsed into silence. He made no mention of his personal life, of his marriage to Cynthia or his purchase of the Priory.

It was with an intense feeling of disappointment that Fleur realised she was to hear no more. Dinner had come to an end. She got to her feet as Barham brought in the coffee.

"I must go to your mother," she said. "Thank you for telling me about the works. I think it is one of the most exciting stories I have ever heard. Perhaps one day you will let me go round the factory. I should be so very interested."

149

For a moment Sir Norman didn't answer; then as she reached the door, he spoke:

"When my mother is shut up for the night, Miss Garton, I wonder if you'd come down to the library for a few minutes? There is something I want to ask you."

"That will be about ten o'clock, Sir Norman."

As Fleur went upstairs, she wondered what he could possibly wish to say to her. Could it be about Anthony?—and yet, even if he disapproved of her behaviour, what could he do? When she was off duty, her time was her own.

Besides, Sir Norman had certainly not seemed disapproving this evening, in fact, she had never known him more conversational, more interesting.

"I don't believe any of these people have ever allowed him to talk," she thought. "That's half the trouble. They've let him become so reserved that he finds it difficult to come out of his shell."

Mrs. Mitcham was waiting for her, the coffee by her bedside.

"You're late," she said accusingly. "Who's been keeping you—the handsome Anthony?"

"No, I haven't seen him this evening," Fleur replied. "Sir Norman was telling me how the works started. I was very interested."

"Works and the works ... that's all he thinks about," Mrs. Mitcham said disdainfully. "At one time it was all motor cars and now it's nothing but aeroplanes."

"But still, they've certainly served their purpose," Fleur said. "Look what Sir Norman's been able to buy with the money he's made from them."

She couldn't help letting her glance linger for a moment on the jewels sparkling round Mrs. Mitcham's withered neck and on her stiff, ugly fingers. Against her quilted bedjacket a fine aquamarine brooch, the stones set in a design of flowers and leaves, sparkled and shone.

"Oh, it has its points," Mrs. Mitcham said, and added unabashed: "I expect you're looking at that brooch. Norman gave me that for my last birthday. Yes, money can buy things like jewels, though, as I told him, he shouldn't be buying them for an old woman like me, but for someone young and pretty."

"Why should he if he doesn't want to?" Fleur said, and was surprised at the sharpness of her tone.

This eternal harping on sex, she thought to herself, was getting on her nerves; it was irritating and unnecessary. Really, when women reached Mrs. Mitcham's age, it was more natural for them to be concerned with religion or the after-life than with the lusts of the flesh.

But Mrs. Mitcham was quite unrebuked. She looked at Fleur and chuckled to herself.

"You're upset—upset and rather irritable. What is it, dearie? You'd better tell me. Has young Anthony been making love to you?"

"I shouldn't tell you if he had," Fleur retorted. "You know too much."

"So he has!" Mrs. Mitcham said, excitedly. "That's what I expected, but don't let Norman catch you. He disapproves of Anthony."

"Why?"

"Well, I've always had my suspicions that he encouraged Cynthia to get up to mischief. He was always hanging about the place and taking her up to London when Norman was busy. Of course, people said they were like brother and sister, still one never knows— human nature being what it is."

"I don't believe that Lady Cynthia liked her cousin that way."

There was no reason for Fleur to make such a remark, it was just that the conviction was strong upon her that Cynthia would not have cared for Anthony as a lover. He was too obvious, too suave for anyone so intelligent and so lovely as Fleur pictured Cynthia in her imagination.

"And what do you know about it?" Mrs. Mitcham asked.

But while Fleur answered humbly, "Nothing, of course," and knew herself snubbed, she remained quite unshaken in her innermost conviction.

It was after ten o'clock when Mrs. Mitcham was finally shut up for the night. Fleur was just making her way to her own room when she remembered Sir Norman had wanted to see her.

"I wonder what it can be," she thought again as she went down to the library. "Perhaps it's the sack, after all. Oh well, who cares?"

She had a wild idea that perhaps Sir Norman had discovered that Anthony had come to her room the night before and was determined to prevent him doing so tonight by keeping her out of the way.

There was no reason to imagine such a thing, but Fleur, as she opened the library door, felt small and insignificant—a schoolgirl approaching the headmaster.

Sir Norman was not at his desk; instead, he was sitting in a big armchair reading. He put down the book as soon as she came into the room and got to his feet.

"Oh, here you are, Miss Garton," he said. "Did my mother expect me to go up and say good night to her?"

"I don't think so," Fleur said.

She remembered uncomfortably that Evans had said:

"I hope to goodness that he doesn't come up here upsetting her again. It'll take her days to get over that last flare-up. It's always the same when they have a set-to of that sort, she'll go on until she's said her say, even if it takes her a month of Sundays."

"No, I'm sure she didn't," Fleur added, wondering if it would be wiser to suggest that he kept away from his mother until she had forgotten the whole episode.

"I'm glad," Sir Norman said. "It's always difficult to know exactly what my mother will be like on these occasions. Sometimes she forgives me at once and then is furious if I am not there to play the penitent; but at other times I'm in her black books for a long time."

He smiled and Fleur found herself smiling in response.

152

"It must be difficult," she agreed sympathetically.

"Won't you sit down?" he asked.

He pointed to the sofa. She sat down rather on the edge, nervously wondering what was coming.

"Do you like being here?" Sir Norman asked abruptly.

The question was unexpected and Fleur found herself hesitating before she found words to reply.

"I admire the house more than I can say," she began, after a pause. "And I like being with your mother. She's very unlike the average old lady of her age."

"That's true enough. She's always been original. Sometimes it has its disadvantages."

Again Sir Norman smiled and there was a twinkle in his eyes. Fleur looked at him in amazement. Why had he altered, she wondered, and what was the point of this conversation.

"I'm glad you're happy here," he went on.

He got up suddenly from his chair and stood with his back to the empty hearth.

"There was something I wanted to say to you." Fleur held her breath. "It is rather awkward for me—I hope you will understand if I seem to be clumsy and untactful."

Fleur felt she knew exactly what was coming. She stiffened a little, feeling already the rising resentment within her. There was silence, then Sir Norman cleared his throat.

"I have forbidden my wife's cousin, Anthony Ashwin, the house."

"On my account?" Fleur asked.

"There are other reasons too, but perhaps that is the one which concerns us at the moment."

"I think you have no right to do that," Fleur said, hotly.

"Haven't I?"

She felt impotent and ineffective.

"I don't think I understand. What are you implying by this?"

"I am not implying anything but I am prepared to

153

state facts. Anthony Ashwin is a rotter and a waster—you are a very attractive young woman. What you do in your spare time is, of course, not my business. As your employer, I am only entitled to ask for your loyalty and your efficiency during working hours.

"But as that same employer and as your host while you are living under my roof, I have no right to subject you to insult or to ask you to meet people who are undesirable."

"Don't you think those are rather strong words?" Fleur asked.

"I could use far stronger where the gentleman in question is concerned," Sir Norman replied grimly.

"But you can't do this. Can't you understand what harm it will do you personally to turn an Ashwin out of the house, especially Captain Anthony who has lived here since he was a child. He knows the place and he loves it—the servants know him and they love him, too. It would cause deep resentment, it would make you hated . . ."

She hesitated. She had been about to say—"more than you are already," and then she realised not only that she must suppress the words themselves, but also that she did not know whether or not they were true.

Was Sir Norman hated? What did the household feel about him? Perhaps, as Anthony had implied, he was just a nonentity, a Midas at whom everyone laughed.

She was conscious that Sir Norman was looking at her strangely.

"And would that worry you?"

"Worry me!" Fleur echoed. "I suppose it's got nothing to do with me, but since you are talking frankly it is obvious that there is something wrong here. You've got this wonderful house, but you are not happy, anyone can see that. You've given your mother everything that money can buy, and yet she'd be happier in less luxurious circumstances.

"Perhaps I'm talking wildly, perhaps I'm being very stupid . . . I expect you will dismiss me after this anyway,

154

so I may as well speak the truth ... but I feel that there's something wrong ... wrong in your life and in hers.

"The only thing that's contented and at peace is the house itself, and that is because of the past ... it has no present."

She heard her voice, raised a little, slightly hysterical, die away, and then with what was almost a sob, she added:

"I'm sorry, Sir Norman, I oughtn't to speak like this."

Norman Mitcham walked across the room and back again; then he stopped beside her and stood looking down.

"You're right," he said, "dead right, I suppose I am unhappy—I think I always have been. But have you considered the solution?"

"The solution?" Fleur asked stupidly.

"I can think of only one," he said, and it seemed as if a grim humour twisted his lips. "It is, of course, that I should get married, that I should have a child to whom I could leave my much vaunted millions. Miss Garton, will you marry me?"

CHAPTER FIFTEEN

"Are you crazy?"

The words came stammeringly from Fleur's lips. She was conscious of feeling hysterical, of wanting to escape, to run away. This must be a dream; it was fantastic, unreal.

"You can't know what you're saying." She heard her voice tremble.

"I'm sorry if it appears like that to you," Sir Norman said quietly, and his tone, steady and unemotional, calmed her.

"Then you really mean . . . ?"

"That I want to marry you? Yes, Miss Garton, and if you will forgive my saying so, I see nothing very strange in the idea. I cannot believe I am the first man who has proposed marriage to you."

"No, but . . . oh, it's just that it is so unexpected, so strange . . ."

"Coming from me?"

"I . . . I had no idea."

"Of course not," Sir Norman said decisively.

Fleur pulled herself together. She did not know why she had experienced that moment of panic, a moment almost of terror.

I must take this calmly, she thought, and knew that her heart was beating, her fingers interlaced tightly so that the knuckles were white.

"It's like this, Miss Garton," Sir Norman went on. "I have known for a long time that things were not right in this house. I also love the Priory—perhaps I have loved it too much, but that's beside the point—but I realise that it needs a mistress, a woman to look after it, perhaps to look after me too."

His smile was almost whimsical, but Fleur was not looking at him, she was staring at the empty hearth, the idea turning over and over in her mind—

"Sir Norman wants to marry you—the Priory could be yours. He is offering it to you, this marvellous, exquisite house."

"I quite understand," he was saying, "that my abrupt approach may be a shock—I'm afraid I'm not very well versed in these things—but you must take my word that I am not making you this offer without due consideration.

"My mother has told me that you have suffered in the past, that things have not planned out as you wished; and I imagined, perhaps presumptuously, that I might be able to offer you a different sort of life, but one which eventually you might find equally as satisfying as that which you have lost."

Fleur made no answer; and after a moment, looking down at her bent head, he continued:

"Our existence here as you've seen it must seem dull, but were you my wife it could be very different. You could invite you own friends to the house, ask them to stay. Hospitality of any sort is, of course, difficult in wartime, but a state of war will not last for ever and then you would be able to enjoy yourself."

"Do you really think that sort of thing interests me?" Fleur asked. "I mean entertaining, having crowds of people about the place?"

"Doesn't it?" Sir Norman inquired. "I thought all women liked people and parties. I always find my own time fully occupied, but I can quite understand that for a woman there are idle hours to be filled and that a young woman needs companions of her own age."

Fleur shuddered. The whole picture sounded false to her. What was he trying to do, she wondered—make marriage to him sound more attractive, offer her such palliatives as a kind of bribe?

It was all so incredible, so beyond the wildest flights of her imagination. She realised that in her silence she was being rude.

"I'm sorry to appear so stupid. It's just that I am trying to get used to the idea that you are really asking me to marry you."

"There's no need for you to give me your answer now. Will you think it over?"

"Yes ... I mean so ... I mean ... Oh, Sir Norman, I must be frank about this. I want you to understand that it is quite impossible."

"Why?" He asked the question abruptly.

Fleur stood up to face him.

"For one thing, I never wish to marry anyone. For another I wouldn't get married unless I was in love."

"Is it possible for you to marry the man you love?"

"No." Fleur answered honestly.

"Then that rules out one objection," Sir Norman said quietly.

She looked at him and saw that there was the glint of battle in his eyes.

He's going to fight me over this, she thought. He's made up his mind and he's determined to gain his ends as he has in everything in his life up to date.

She felt an almost detached amusement at the thought, at the idea of defying so powerful and determined a man.

"Your other objection," Sir Norman went on, "that you will never get married, is surely a statement made without thought or consideration. You are young and, as I have already said, very attractive. You are also, I understand, not well off. It is easy now to earn your own living, there will always be posts open to you; but have you thought of your later life, of your old age?

"Poverty can be hard and very uncomfortable then. The day that I marry you I shall settle a sum sufficient to bring you in an independent income whatever happens to me or to our marriage in the future."

"You are making what ought to be a very attractive proposition," Fleur said, "but somehow I can't imagine myself accepting it."

"That's frank, at any rate, and may I ask why?"

"One can't enter into marriage as if it was a business deal."

"A large number of people do."

"Perhaps . . . but they sugar the pill."

"Haven't I sugared it sufficiently?"

"I can't make you understand," Fleur said in despair. "Really, Sir Norman, I think it would be far better if we stopped talking like this. Can't we forget about . . . this . . . this proposal? I like looking after your mother, and I like being at the Priory, but I can't stay unless we remain as we were . . . erase this conversation altogether."

"That's impossible," Sir Norman answered, "and you know it as well as I do. What's been said can't be unsaid. But there's no reason for you to feel awkward or embarrassed. My offer remains open indefinitely. I have already asked you to think it over. Please don't give me any answer now—I prefer to wait."

She felt there was no more to say; she felt too as if he dismissed her, yet somehow she could not leave things as they were. Womanlike, she forgot her shyness and sense of embarrassment in an overwhelming curiosity.

"There's one thing I would like to know," she said. "In showing me the many advantages of being your wife you haven't told me the real reason why you require one. Is it because you are lonely or because you need an heir?"

A strange expression crossed Sir Norman's face. She couldn't read it, couldn't understand what it meant. Then, in a voice flat and unmoved, he replied:

"I would like a child of mine to carry on the business, to inherit this house, but I am prepared to wait for that."

Fleur had the impression that he had something more to say; then, as they stood there, she had the strange feeling that he too was shy. Again she could not hold back a question which demanded to be asked.

"And supposing you have no children, who will inherit the Priory when you are dead?"

He made a little gesture—she was not certain if it was one of impatience or indifference.

"It is mine unconditionally; I can leave it to whom I please."

"It ought to go to an Ashwin."

"Why?"

Now he looked aggressive and she knew she had annoyed him.

"Because there have always been Ashwins here," she replied. "I have been reading their history. I feel the very stones must be impregnated with Ashwin blood; everything—the building, the furniture, the pictures are all part of the Ashwin inheritance."

"Yet now it's mine." It seemed to her that Norman Mitcham almost shouted the words. "Mine, to do with as I like."

He walked across the room and back again, then stood looking at a picture which hung above the mantelpiece, a conversation piece of the fifth earl grouped with his wife and children in the gardens. Behind them stood the Priory.

"I remember the first time I saw this house," Norman Mitcham said, his eyes on the picture; "I was poaching, trying with two other ragged lads to snare a rabbit or a pheasant for our suppers. It was evening and as we came out of the woods, those which lie to the north of the drive, we saw below us the Priory."

He stopped. There was a long pause.

"Yes?" Fleur prompted. "What did you feel?"

"I think from that moment I meant to own it," Norman Mitcham replied. He turned to face her. "You said just now there was something wrong in my life. I don't know quite what you meant by that. I have, it is true, lost my wife. We were unsuited to each other; I was a fool to have thought that we could ever be anything else; but I have gained a certain position, at least in the world of industry, and I have the Priory. Do you still imagine there is something wrong?"

"You do not seem a happy man. Are you? Can you honestly say that you have found happiness?"

"What is happiness?" Sir Norman asked. "If it is doing a good job of work and knowing that one has given one's best—then I am happy. If it is achieving one's ambition, then also I am happy."

He spoke defiantly, and she guessed that he was trying to convince her against an inner conviction that she was right.

"But you are lonely," she said quickly. "You must be lonely."

"If you think that, why not make me happy by doing what I want?"

"That's evading the question," she parried; and for the first time she felt at ease with him, more natural, less agitated. "You are lonely, you know that. What sort of life do you lead? You work all day and come home to sit alone in the evenings. What do you think about then? Do you read or is your mind still turning over the problems of the factory?"

He hesitated for a moment and she felt that he debated with himself whether he should tell the truth; then with a smile which she knew with a flash of intuition to be an expression of extreme shyness, he said:

"I'll be honest with you. I'm educating myself. I've never had much time for learning, you see, so I sit here in the evenings reading. Sometimes I must confess I fall asleep over my lessons."

"What do you read?"

Again he hesitated and then replied:

"Well, mostly the *Encyclopaedia Britannica.* That

seems to me to give a pretty comprehensive survey of all that a person should know."

For a moment Fleur longed to laugh, there was something so preposterous in the idea of any man sitting down to read the whole of the *Encyclopaedia Britannica* in search of knowledge, and then quite suddenly the pathos of it struck her.

This man of all men, a man whose name was a household word for efficiency and progress.

"Perhaps," she said gently, "I could help you. My father had a big library and all my life I have been brought up amongst books. I could, perhaps, recommend more interesting and less cumbersome reading of the subjects which interest you."

"I don't think you understand," Sir Norman said impatiently. "I don't know what subjects to choose. Have you ever thought what it would be like to leave school at twelve; to work with your hands, day after day, year after year, to stop only when one was so tired that one could go no longer without sleep; to know and talk only with people who laboured as one did oneself?

"Then, out of life, to step suddenly into the Priory, to be surrounded by things which one knows instinctively are beautiful, but which one cannot appreciate because of an abysmal ignorance?

"In my works I can command respect form my employees, I know more than they do; but here, in the Priory, a housemaid or Barham knows more than I—or rather, they did. I think I can flatter myself that I have at least equalled, even surpassed, their knowledge by now."

There was a note, not of triumph, but of pain in his voice.

"Something has hurt him," Fleur thought; "someone has put that idea into his head. It is not original."

Could it have been Cynthia, she wondered, or maybe Anthony with his sneering references to asses' ears? Had Norman known about that?

Quite suddenly a picture of the past seemed clear, the

pieces which had come singly to her mind fell together like a jigsaw puzzle, making a complete whole. Cynthia's friends, her relations like Anthony, laughing and sneering at Norman, finding him common, gauche and uneducated.

Fleur could imagine him knowing what they were saying, suffering from their gibes, steeling himself to silence lest he should betray to them his ignorance of all they knew instinctively by birth and position.

Lady Cynthia Ashwin, of the proud, defiant eyes! The idea of Sir Norman being married to her seemed stranger than ever now. Of course they had been unhappy.

Fleur could see that pictured face with its fine, aristocratic features looking out on life fastidiously. Lady Cynthia and the boy who had been the "boots" at the Priory—what a marriage for the last owner of that great house!

Why had she done it? And having made the bargain, why had she broken it?

Then, as she thought of Cynthia Ashwin, Fleur knew that deeper than all her other reasons for refusing to consider marriage with Sir Norman was the feeling that he was still married . . .

Abruptly, he broke in on her thoughts.

"Of what are you thinking?"

"I was thinking about you and your wife."

"I divorced her," he said gruffly.

"I know."

"Are you religious?"

"If you mean by that, do I go to Church a great deal? . . . the answer is no. If you mean, is my faith in God a real thing? . . . the answer is yes."

"You wouldn't consider that I had divorced my wife a bar to remarriage?"

"I don't know," Fleur said, afraid to tell him the truth.

*　　*　　*

It was only when she was alone in her room after this amazing interview that she faced the fact that the thought of taking Cynthia's place at the Priory seemed almost like sacrilege to her.

In the short time she had been there she had imagined so much about it's former mistress; now the idea of supplanting her was almost more fantastic than the idea of marrying Sir Norman himself.

Once she had searched the house for traces of Lady Cynthia; now it seemed to Fleur as if everything in the place was a part of her.

The portraits of the Ashwins on the staircase, each in its own way, recalled Cynthia; the furniture and furnishings, the rooms in which she had lived since she was a child, each had known her, each had been a background for her development.

"It is as impossible to escape from her as it is to escape from the feeling that we are interlopers," Fleur thought.

And she saw once again how pitiable Sir Norman's aspirations were. He could never in his lifetime attempt to catch up with all that the Ashwins had evolved over centuries.

Fleur felt that she could cry at the sadness and the waste of it—a man eating out his heart to attain the dilettante graces and airs which come from the breeding of generations.

For that, she knew, was at the bottom of Sir Norman's desire for education; he wanted deep within himself, whether he admitted it or not, to achieve the poise and self-confidence of an Ashwin.

How impossible, how utterly impossible it was for him, and how still more impossible to imagine herself helping and guiding him, taking her place beside him for the rest of their lives!

She thought of Jack and how she had loved him; she thought of what had seemed to her the miracle of their love across the Channel in enemy-shadowed France.

Then, remembering her own disillusionment, her unhappiness, those bitter anguished nights of loneliness and yearning, she saw the Priory as she had first seen it that day she was walked up the drive to interview Mrs. Mitcham.

That breathtaking perfection could be hers!

And then she corrected the thought. The Priory could never belong to anyone but the Ashwins; but she could at least have the privilege of living in it, of being a custodian for her life of its beauty and treasures.

But there was also Sir Norman!

She had grown used to finding him so morose and unresponsive that she had imagined him to be only a driving force for his own chariot wheels.

Now she saw him as a man, sensitive and introspective, who could be hurt cruelly and irrevocably. She thought of the nights that she had cried in utter misery and wondered if Sir Norman had suffered as she had.

She longed to know what he had endured during the years of his marriage; yet she had the uneasy feeling that he would never speak to her openly of Cynthia.

When she had mentioned her name, she had felt at once as if Sir Norman had withdrawn into himself, as if the tentative advances he was making in inviting her confidence and giving her his were instantly repulsed.

After she had spoken of his marriage, the conversation had been more stilted, it had been difficult to recapture again that moment of intimacy when he had told her of his desire to educate himself and of what he was reading.

Only when finally she had said good night had the barriers dropped again and he had taken her hand, holding it for a second in his firm fingers.

"You will think over what I have asked you? There is no need for you to give your answer now or for a long time."

"It is really impossible, Sir Norman," Fleur said, struggling with the feeling that he was overwhelming her, driving her into a corner, and that somehow she could not escape from him.

"Nothing is impossible."

"In which case shall we say it is very improbable."

"That's better," he said; "I feel I have gained a point."

Fleur had to smile.

"You frighten me."

He let go her hand and straightened his shoulders.

"I promise you I will never force you to do anything against your will."

"Thank you."

Then, as she turned towards the door, Sir Norman added:

"But I always try to get my own way."

He said it light-heartedly, almost boyishly, and she replied:

"I have heard that. You've got rather a formidable reputation. Did you know they call you the juggernaut?"

Norman Mitcham grinned and for a moment looked quite young. She heard him chuckle to himself as she shut the library door behind her and went across the hall and upstairs.

Only as she reached her own room did she feel half-afraid, wondering whether he would achieve this ambition as he had achieved all the other things in life on which he had set his heart.

The story of how he had seen the Priory for the first time had been strangely moving. She thought of that small boy looking at the beauty of the old grey house, at the lake with its black swans—the whole tale with its Cinderella-ending of ultimate possession, was one to inspire amazement and envy, and yet Fleur did not envy him.

Their conversation had only increased her conviction that he was unhappy, that there was something wrong in the household.

"And how could I put it right?" she asked herself.

Could she bring Norman Mitcham happiness? She

knew it was impossible without love, and then, accusingly, she saw the truth and shrank from it.

Already, deep within herself, she was contemplating marrying a man, not because she wanted him, but because she loved and desired the house in which he lived.

CHAPTER SIXTEEN

Fleur, looking for Barham, found him, not in the pantry, but in the big dining-room with all the silver-plate spread out on the table.

"Sir Norman has telephoned and asked me to tell you that Melchester was very badly bombed last night," Fleur told him. "We may be asked to house some of the people who are homeless."

Barham put down his silver-brush with decision.

"We don't want them here and that's that, making a mess of the carpets, mucking up the place."

"But, Barham," Fleur exclaimed, "just think of what they are suffering. I could hear the bombs in the distance all night—I expect they kept you awake too—and there was a great red glow in the sky."

"I'm sorry for them," Barham admitted grudgingly; "at the same time there's other places better suited to take them in than the Priory."

"I expect every house in Melford will have somebody; that's if the damage is as bad as Sir Norman thinks. At any rate, he asks you to be prepared."

The bombing of the night before had been, Fleur guessed, particularly severe, even before she had heard the facts from Sir Norman.

Melchester was about twelve miles away from the Priory, and the bombs had shaken the house, making the windows rattle and rendering sleep impossible, at any rate for Sir Norman and Fleur. Mrs. Mitcham had not been unduly disturbed.

"I heard the devils," she said, "but I says to myself—'Lying awake won't do anybody any good and only give them satisfaction if they knew of it'—so I went to sleep again."

Fleur wished that she had had such command over her senses.

She had lain shuddering at every impact, afraid, not for yourself, but for the people who were being killed, maimed or rendered homeless, by the savagery and terror of death raining from the skies.

Now she walked to the library and at that moment the telephone on Sir Norman's desk rang. Fleur wondered if she should answer it.

Usually Sir Norman's secretary was here by this time, a quiet, middle-aged woman who attended both to his personal correspondence at the office and to the household accounts at the Priory.

Apparently, Miss Shaw had been detained. Fleur picked up the receiver and answered the telephone herself.

"Who is it speaking?"

"Can I speak to Sir Norman Mitcham?" asked a female voice.

"I'm afraid he is not here. Can I give him a message?"

"I must get in touch with him."

"You will find him at the works; at least, he is on his way there. You will get him in another ten minutes."

There was a moment's hesitation and then the woman said:

"I wonder if you could help me? You see, it's rather difficult to get a line. I'm speaking from the outskirts of Melchester."

"I'll do anything I can," Fleur said warmly.

"It's Nurse Thompson speaking. I am nurse to Lady Cynthia Ashwin. The sanatorium in which she was staying was bombed last night."

"Is she hurt?" Fleur asked the question quickly.

"No, luckily none of the patients were injured, but we have had to get them away from the sanatorium and Lady Cynthia is most insistent that she should be taken at once to Greystone Priory. We have already ordered a car, but I thought it would be wiser to ring through first and warn Sir Norman to expect us."

"I will tell Sir Norman," Fleur said. "In the meantime, Lady Cynthia's room will be got ready."

"Oh, thank you so much."

She heard the relief in the nurse's voice and knew that she had been embarrassed at the task which had been assigned to her.

"What time shall we expect you?"

"I think we should be there within an hour or so. I shall be coming alone with Lady Cynthia as, for the moment, another nurse cannot be spared, but she really requires a night nurse."

"I will see if I can get one. Is she very ill?"

"I'm afraid so, and last night has been an unpleasant experience."

"Of course."

Fleur said good-bye and put down the receiver; then she stood for a moment feeling strangely moved. So Cynthia Ashwin was coming home! What would Sir Norman say? What would everyone in the household say?

While she stood there, the door opened and Miss Shaw bustled in. Fleur told her what had occurred and asked her to break the news to Sir Norman. Miss Shaw looked startled.

"I don't know what Sir Norman will say to such a thing. Suppose he refuses to have her?"

"Oh, he couldn't!" Fleur replied. "How could he? The sanatorium's been bombed, she's ill . . . desperately ill . . . and she wants to come here. I'll go and get her room ready. You'd better telephone Sir Norman at the works."

"I wish you'd do it," Miss Shaw said apprehensively.

"I haven't the time," Fleur replied, and hurried upstairs.

She called Manvers and told her to open up the closed room in the west wing and get it ready at once. She hardly waited to hear the housemaid's expressions of astonishment before she sped away to Mrs. Mitcham.

The old lady was in the process of making up her face, an operation which took a long time every morning after Evans had got her bathed and dressed up in a freshly curled wig.

Fleur broke the news quietly; but as she had expected, Mrs. Mitcham received it with great excitement.

"Cynthia coming here!" she exclaimed. "Well, that's queer, I must say. And you say she's ill. Well, I should have thought there'd be plenty of other places she could have gone to, but I suppose it's natural—the Priory will always be home to her, Norman or no Norman about the place. But what's he going to say to this?"

"I'm sure Sir Norman will feel it is only right that Lady Cynthia should find refuge here," Fleur said quickly. "He was expecting that we should have some of the homeless from Melchester sent to us."

"He didn't expect that one of them would be his own wife, I'll be bound," Mrs. Mitcham said. "Well, it'll save us from being dull—eh, Evans?"

"Now don't excite yourself," Evans said sharply. "You know what the doctor said. Besides, if you get a bad attack, we shall have to shut you up and you'll hear nothing and see nobody. So take things calmly."

"Don't croak at me, you old crow," Mrs. Mitcham retorted. "You make me feel ill, always fussing and fretting. For heaven's sake, woman, let me die the way I want to!"

Fleur had to laugh; then she hurried away to tell Mrs. Jackson there would be extra for luncheon and to break the news to Barham. He was still in the dining-room, engrossed in his silver cleaning. Fleur could not help feeling the drama of the moment as she said gently:

"Lady Cynthia Ashwin is on her way here, Barham. The sanatorium in which she had been staying has been bombed. She and the nurse are coming here immediately."

She had never seen the old man look so pleased. As he put down the big silver sauceboat that he was polishing, she saw that his hands were shaking.

"It'll be like old times to see her ladyship again," he said, "just like old times."

Her errands finished, Fleur went into the garden and picked a huge bowl of pink roses for Cynthia's room. There was no time to wait for carnations to be brought from the hot-houses which were some distance away.

The roses were perfect and Fleur carried them upstairs and placed them on the long, marble-topped dressing-table so that Cynthia could see them from her bed.

Manvers and an under-housemaid were busy preparing the room, the blinds were up, the windows were open, and the lavender-scented linen sheets with their big embroidered monograms were being put on the bed.

Long before they were ready, Fleur heard the sound of a car drawing up at the front door and guessed that Cynthia had arrived.

She ran to the top of the stairs; she saw Barham cross the hall, his usual slow pompous gait accelerated so that he went almost at a run; the front door was opened and there was the sound of voices.

Then she saw them bringing in a stretcher.

Somehow she had not expected this, it was so unlike the picture she had in her own mind of Cynthia Ashwin. A stretcher!

There was something almost frightening in the men moving slowly and the still figure covered in blankets. Fleur watched them cross the hall and then, as they paused before negotiating the stairs, she heard a clear voice say:

"Well, Barham, you see they have brought me home to die."

172

She hardly heard Barham's answer, her eyes were fixed on the head raised on a pillow, the dark hair brushed back from a square forehead, the pointed chin resting on the enveloping blankets. Slowly the men carrying the stretcher reached the top of the stairs and Fleur, standing aside, saw Cynthia Ashwin for the first time.

"She's old," was her first quick, disappointed impression, and then—"but she's lovely ... still lovely."

She was conscious of Cynthia's eyes looking at her questioningly as she hurried forward to direct the men along the passage to the west wing. Cynthia was carried into her own room.

Manvers was waiting, and as the men who had carried the stretcher withdrew, Fleur went with them. Tactfully she felt that for the moment she must leave Cynthia alone—alone with those who had known her.

After a few minutes Nurse Thompson came out of the room. Fleur held out her hand.

"I am Miss Garton," she said. "You spoke to me on the telephone. Would your patient like anything?"

"Nothing for the moment, thank you," Nurse Thompson replied. "She stood the journey well. But she's rather over-excited, I'm afraid. It's the idea of coming here. She talked about her home so often, you see. I've been with her for a long time and I feel as if I know every stick and stone of the place already."

Fleur showed the nurse her room which was next door; then, feeling there was nothing more she could do, she turned to go downstairs. As she reached the staircase, Manvers came hurrying after her.

"Her ladyship would like to speak to you. She asked who you were."

Fleur went back to Cynthia's room. She knocked and felt suddenly shy when Nurse Thompson opened the door. She walked across the long stretch of carpet to the foot of the bed.

Cynthia was lying back against her pillows, her hands lying limply on the white sheets. She was dreadfully emaciated, the bones of her wrists sharp and prominent; her neck, too, was painfully thin and wasted.

Fleur realised how very much older Cynthia was than she had ever imagined her to be. Always she had thought of her as a young, joyous girl and pictured her as she had appeared in the photograph album.

Now she saw that Cynthia was over forty, her skin wasted and lined by illness, yet even so she was lovely.

Her face was still exquisitely heart-shaped; her eyes, abnormally large in contrast to her sunken cheeks, were dark and lustrous; her lips still full and curved, and when she smiled Fleur thought that she had a charm that was indescribable.

"I don't think we have met." Cynthia was speaking; her voice had a lilting quality of its own.

"I am Fleur Garton. I'm housekeeper and companion to Mrs. Mitcham."

"So Manvers tells me. I am sorry if I have upset you by my precipitate arrival."

"I only hope you will have everything you want."

"It's everything just to be back. It was good of you to give me my own room. I was half-afraid someone else would be using it."

"No one has used it," Fleur said. "It's always been kept shut up."

She knew that this was what Cynthia had wanted to know and she could tell that she was pleased; but she said nothing, only looked round the room, glancing at the furniture, the chandelier, the silk curtains moving slowly in the breeze, as if caressing them one by one.

"The house hasn't changed much," she said at length and then added, "but you wouldn't know. Have you been here long?"

Fleur told her.

"How is Mrs. Mitcham?"

"She is fairly well, but she is bedridden."

"So there will be two of us," Cynthia said reflectively. "Two women waiting to die in the house."

"But you mustn't," Fleur said quickly.

174

"Mustn't die?" Cynthia smiled. "My dear child, I'm looking forward to it. And now I have come home it will have to be quick before I am turned out again."

"Don't talk like that, please. There couldn't be any question of . . ."

Fleur stopped, wondering what she could possibly say, what right she had to say it.

"We mustn't forget Norman, must we?" Cynthia asked, and both her words and her smile included Fleur, allying her on her side, two women against a man.

But Fleur felt a sudden loyalty, a quick-springing desire to stand up for Norman, to speak for him.

"Sir Norman," she said with emphasis, "is delighted that you have come here."

She sensed rather than saw the surprise in Cynthia's eyes as she turned away, making her way back towards the door. Cynthia made no effort to stop her, and when she was outside in the passage again, Fleur knew that her heart was beating rapidly.

Without stopping to think she ran along the passage and down the stairs. She must find Miss Shaw in the library and hear what Sir Norman had said when he had been told the news.

And then, as she reached the hall, she saw him coming in through the front door. He was walking briskly, pulling off the gloves he habitually wore for driving.

"Well, what is it?" he asked irritably.

Fleur stood and looked at him.

"Is my mother ill?" he inquired. "Well, can't you answer me? I've got a busy morning. To be brought back here by these cryptic telephone messages is no joke. What has happened?"

Then Fleur understood. So Miss Shaw had funked it, had been too afraid to tell him the truth and had merely brought him back with an urgent telephone message.

"There was no need for you to have returned before luncheon," she said quietly. "I asked Miss Shaw to telephone you and tell you that Lady Cynthia Ashwin, having been bombed out and having nowhere to go, was coming here from Melchester Sanatorium."

Sir Norman was very still, Fleur thought that the lines round his mouth were more pronounced than ever. Quite suddenly she was afraid.

"But it's impossible. . . ."

She interrupted him almost before the words left his lips.

"Lady Cynthia is here," she said quickly; "she arrived a few minutes ago. She is very ill and very glad to be back. She is only afraid that you will not allow her to stay."

"She's afraid of that, is she?"

"And I told her that you were very glad to have her."

Sir Norman turned and looked at Fleur.

"Why did you say that?"

"Because you are," Fleur insisted. "Of course you are glad to have her—you've got to be. Don't you understand, she's come home."

She stood looking at him as if she would impress her will upon him; and then, as she waited, hardly daring to breathe lest he should fail her, lest he should do what she feared rather than what she anticipated, Sir Norman put out his hand and touched her shoulder.

"Thank you, Fleur," he said gravely. "Yes, I am pleased for Cynthia to be here."

He walked past her into the library, shutting the door behind him. Fleur put up her hands and covered her eyes for a moment.

It has been a battle into which she had flung every ounce of her willpower, all the strength of her resolution.

Now that she had attained victory she felt curiously weak.

CHAPTER SEVENTEEN

"Her ladyship wants you."

Fleur, hurrying along the passage to Cynthia's room, wondered how many times in the last few days she had heard this request.

Cynthia appeared to have taken a liking to her and she found herself being sent for continually. Sometimes it was something Cynthia required from the garden or the library, at others it was just a desire to chat.

She was indeed, as the doctors confirmed, a very ill woman. It wrung Fleur's heart to see her so frail, to watch those agonising fits of coughing which left her each time more exhausted and at times almost prostrate after a severe haemorrhage.

Fleur's position these days was a strange one. She was with Cynthia for a large part of the day and then in the evening she would dine with Sir Norman.

The nurses had their meals upstairs in the sitting-room set aside for their exclusive use. Fleur would be alone with her host. He was always very quiet and it was difficult to know what he was thinking and feeling about the situation.

Since Cynthia's arrival he had never referred in any way to his own future or to Fleur's. The conversation in which he had asked her to marry him might, as she had suggested, really have been erased from their memories.

At times she was slightly piqued, wondering if indeed

he had forgotten, if he had changed his mind and no longer wanted her for his wife.

Naturally, at such a moment, with Cynthia in the house, it was impossible to contemplate such a step; nevertheless, womanlike, Fleur wanted to probe into Sir Norman's feelings, to know what he was thinking.

She had actually been present when he had seen Cynthia for the first time since her arrival. It had been a moment undramatic and unemotional. She had been in Cynthia's bedroom with the dinner menu when there had come a knock at the door.

Nurse Thompson had gone to open it and a moment later she had crossed the room to say to Cynthia in a low voice:

"Sir Norman wishes to know if you would like to see him."

"But of course. Ask him to come in."

Fleur turned away, but Cynthia stopped her.

"Don't go, Miss Garton, we haven't decided yet which of Mrs. Johnson's delicious dishes shall tempt my appetite tonight."

She smiled as she spoke, but Fleur imagined there was an appeal in her eyes as if she did not wish to be alone with Norman and begged her support.

He came into the room, moving awkwardly to the bedside. Fleur felt she had never noticed before how ungainly were his movements.

Then she realised that he was embarrassed, shy and awkward in the present of the woman to whom he had once been married. Cynthia waited until he stood beside her, then she put out her hand.

"Thank you for taking in a refugee, Norman. Am I being a nuisance?"

"Of course not. I am very glad to see you." He spoke gravely.

"I've been a wandering Jew, but at last I've reached home."

"I hope—to stay."

Cynthia smiled at him.

"That's kind of you, Norman."

"You have everything you want?—Miss Garton will see to that."

"Miss Garton and everyone have been most kind."

"I am glad."

They exchanged a few more commonplace remarks before Norman excused himself. Fleur had felt disappointed and then was annoyed with herself for being so. What had she expected? What, indeed, had she wanted?

She felt as if she was watching a play—a play which unfolded itself so skilfully that never for one moment could the audience anticipate the next move or the ultimate solution of the plot.

*　　*　　*

Fleur turned the handle of Cynthia's door and went in. It was a grey day and Cynthia had switched on her bedside lamp, so that a soft pink radiance shone on her pillows and on her face. It was easy to see now how beautiful she had been, even while she was but a shadowy echo of that radiant, vivid self.

"Come in, Fleur, I want you."

"What is it?"

"Nothing very important, but Nurse Thompson has gone for a walk—her usual time off. I can't sleep and I'm bored with myself. Come and gossip with me."

"I oughtn't to, really; I've got a lot to do."

"Nonsense! The old woman's asleep, surely, at this hour?"

"Yes, Mrs. Mitcham is taking her rest, but I haven't done the flowers downstairs and Manvers is waiting for me to check the linen."

"Let her wait," Cynthia said impatiently. "How I hate domesticity! It always bored me."

"Well, I'll play truant for once, but if Sir Norman is annoyed with me I shall make you the excuse." Fleur said the last words in deliberate provocation and in just retribution received the last answer she expected.

"From all accounts, Norman is not at all likely to be annoyed with you," Cynthia remarked.

The underlying meaning of her tone, the accent on the pronoun, brought the blood flooding into Fleur's cheeks.

"What do you mean?" she stammered.

Cynthia laughed.

"I've been listening to servants' gossip," she explained. Then smiling at Fleur's embarrassment she went on: "Don't look so horrified. I'm delighted if it's true."

"What have you heard?" Fleur asked quickly.

"I'm being rather mean, really," Cynthia said impulsively. "I've set a trap for you and you've fallen into it. It was horrid of me, Fleur, but you mustn't be angry."

"Won't you explain?"

"Well, the truth is that Barham told Evans, and Evans told Mrs. Mitcham who told Manvers who mentioned it to Nurse Thompson that he wouldn't be surprised to see you walking up the aisle with Norman one of these fine days."

She laughed like a child, having checked off the names on her fingers as she said them.

"Quite frankly, I didn't believe it. I just made the remark to see what you'd say, but I'm afraid your face has given you away."

Fleur struggled to preserve her dignity.

"Sir Norman did suggest something of the sort some time ago, but I told him such a thing was impossible."

"Oh, but why?"

Fleur looked at her curiously.

"Do you think we ought to discuss this?"

"Whyever not?" Cynthia asked. "Do you mean because Norman was my husband? My dear, a lot of water's passed under the bridge since then. I should be delighted if he married again and yet, to be frank, somehow the possibility never occurred to me."

"Why not?"

180

Cynthia shrugged her thin shoulders.

"Norman doesn't seem the marrying sort. He never did."

"And yet you married him."

Fleur spoke without thinking, then wondered if her words sounded impertinent.

"There was a good reason—you know that, of course."

"To save the Priory?"

"Exactly. Not the Priory itself—I wouldn't have had to part with that—but all that was in it. I had no money to keep it up. It meant that the pictures would have to go, the silver, the gold plate, the first editions ... I couldn't bear it ... I couldn't face the prospect. It would have been like the Chinese torture of cutting off one's limbs one by one. And so I gambled and ... lost everything."

"I've often wondered how you could do that."

"I've wondered myself. You can't imagine what it's like to be back here again, to come home, to see all the things I loved around me. When I was out in Kenya, I used to dream of the gardens in spring when the daffodils are golden in the park and I used to shut my eyes and pretend I was looking at the rhododendrons in the woods behind the house. Did you see them this year? They must be over now."

"Yes, I saw them," Fleur said gently.

"Then I used to imagine I was walking through the house, up the staircase, along the gallery, looking at the pictures and the furniture. When I had a nightmare, it was to see the walls empty, the windows broken and the Priory deserted."

"You love it so much," Fleur said softly, "and yet ... you left it."

"I had to," Cynthia said. "I had to."

There was a throb in her voice. Fleur waited, but she said no more. They sat in silence for a few minutes and

181

then with obvious deliberation Cynthia changed the conversation.

"How do you get on with Mrs. Mitcham?" she asked . . .

* * *

It was of the old lady Fleur was thinking as she went downstairs that evening to dinner. Sir Norman was waiting for her in the library, and the moment after she had greeted him Barham announced that dinner was served.

While they were eating the first course Fleur asked:

"Do you think you could speak to your mother? She's being a little difficult and she won't take 'no' for an answer from me."

"What about?"

"She wants to visit Lady Cynthia. We have all told her it is impossible either for her to be moved or for Lady Cynthia to have visitors, but she insists. She has given orders for a wheeled chair to be brought up to her room and I'm afraid that whatever Evans or I say she will insist on trying to get into it."

"The best thing is to forbid the servants to bring one upstairs," Sir Norman suggested.

"That makes things so awkward," Fleur replied. "If she gives an order and you countermand it, things are uncomfortable all round. Perhaps if you reasoned with her . . . I'm afraid I've failed."

"I'll speak to her," Sir Norman promised.

He came up to see his mother just as she was retiring for the night. Fleur left them alone, hoping that the conversation would not end in one of their violent disagreements. She was reading in her own sitting-room when there came a knock at her door.

"Come in," she said, expecting one of the housemaids.

To her surprise it was Sir Norman. It was the first time he had been to her room. She got up quickly, but coming into the room and shutting the door behind him he said:

"Don't move. I don't want to disturb you. I only wanted to tell you the result of my intercession."

"Were you successful?"

"Not very, I'm afraid: but at least she's agreed not to attempt it until Cynthia is stronger. I'm not certain, though, that she means to keep her promise."

"Sometimes it's easy to see where you get your determination."

She spoke lightly and laughed, but to her surprise Sir Norman did not respond. Instead, he said heavily:

"Do you think I am like my mother?"

"I see no resemblance at all," Fleur replied, "except in this one particular."

She felt for no apparent reason that he was relieved. He took out his cigarette-case.

"May I smoke?"

"Of course, and won't you sit down?"

She felt a little embarrassed, flustered by Sir Norman's unexpected presence. She had never imagined him in her room, and while it had seemed easy to entertain Anthony Ashwin there, she felt now a restraint as if she was doing something outrageous. He lit a cigarette and sat down in an armchair.

"My mother is very fond of you," he said. "You are the only person who has ever been able, if not to manage her, to keep her exuberance to a certain extent within bounds."

"She is wonderful for her age."

"She never seems to me to have altered very much. She's always been the same—full of vitality, enthusiasm and an unremittingly aggressive spirit."

Fleur looked startled at the last words.

"Yes, I mean what I say," Sir Norman added, although she had made no remark. "My mother has always been aggressive. Ever since I was a child I remember rows, quarrels, difficulties wherever we went."

"Did you mind?"

He leant forward to flick his ash into the empty grate.

"I hated it."

There was a raw edge to his voice which said even more than his words. Fleur felt herself tense. Sir Norman was beginning to talk to her again. She almost prayed that she might do the right thing to encourage him.

"Children are peculiarly sensitive to atmosphere," she said.

"Yes, I suppose children are; I was, at any rate. But I wonder if you or anyone else could have any idea of the hell my childhood was."

He didn't look at her, but down at his hands. Fleur held her breath.

"I think I must have been very young when I realised how other women scorned my mother. I suppose every boy wants to admire his parents, wants to feel that his home is something to boast about, to be proud of. I was ashamed, bitterly ashamed—of mine.

"My father was lazy and good-humoured—my mother was neither. I think she loved him in her own way despite the fact that she was consistently unfaithful to him.

"When things were too obvious for him to ignore, he took action which consisted in knocking down the man she was with, bringing her home and beating her. I remember cowering in the corner while they flew at each other like a couple of tiger-cats, she screaming and yelling so that the whole neighbourhood was roused.

"The jeers that I received from other children next day made me ashamed. Not that I let them know that I minded. I fought every boy in the place who had a word to say about my mother, and I'm proud to remember that I won the majority of the fights.

"I appeared defiant—at least I think I did; but I suffered terribly. She didn't know, of course. She's always been the same, natural, unaffected, ready to enjoy everything that life could bring her and a good deal that it didn't. But when I . . ."

Norman stopped abruptly. He stubbed out the stump of his cigarette in an ashtray.

"I'm talking too much," he said, "it must be very boring for you."

"But it isn't!" Fleur exclaimed. "I like knowing about your life, surely you can understand that?"

"I can't, really. I've never considered myself particularly interesting. Besides, it's getting late, you'll be going to bed."

"I'm not tired. Please go on talking to me," Fleur pleaded; but she knew it was useless to ask him.

Something had swept the moment of intimacy away and after a few more commonplace sentences he said good night and she was alone.

What had stopped him? she wondered. Had he been going to speak of his marriage? Had the thought of Cynthia being in the house made him check the words as they came to his lips?

His abruptness was bewildering, and yet Fleur knew she had been nearer to the real Norman Mitcham that night than ever before. When he had spoken of his childhood, it was not only what he said, but the expression in his voice that told her the barrier of reserve was falling.

"He's beginning to trust me," she thought, and was startled to find how glad the thought made her. "If I made him more human I shall at least have achieved something during my stay here."

Had he ever told Cynthia what he had told her that evening, she wondered. Had Cynthia known his innermost secrets, the miseries he had suffered as a child and the ambitions which had grown out of them?

She could begin to understand so well why he had coveted the Priory. The poignant contrast of what he had and was, and what he wanted to have and to be!

Norman deserved his success; it was just, it was right that he should have achieved it. The idea came to Fleur that the perfect ending to everything would be for him to be reunited with Cynthia.

Yet even as she considered it, she knew that the idea was fantastic. Cynthia was a dying woman—apart from that it was obvious to the merest outsider that she and Norman could have nothing in common.

While she was sitting there thinking of Norman and of the woman who had been his wife, there came another knock at her door. Fleur's mind leapt to the idea that it might be Norman returning; but when she called "Come in," Nurse Thompson put her head round the door.

"I wondered if you'd gone to bed."

"No, come in, Nurse."

"I was just going off myself. My patient's sleeping like a lamb, and anyway the night nurse is with her."

"She's had a good day, hasn't she?"

"Extraordinarily good for her. Can I have a cigarette?"

"Help yourself, of course."

Nurse Thompson did so and sat down in the armchair recently vacated by Norman. She stretched out her legs and yawned.

"I'm tired! It takes it out of you—nursing."

"I'm sure it does," Fleur sympathised.

"Not that this isn't a good place. I've been with Lady Cynthia now for five or six years. She only went into the sanatorium on condition they'd let her bring her own nurse. I was in Switzerland with her before that and for a short time in Kenya."

"She's had it as long as that, then."

"Oh, yes, she was bad when I came to her, but she was unhappy too, and that doesn't help in any illness."

"Was that over the man who was killed?"

Nurse Thompson nodded.

"It happened some time before, but she was still suffering. It was terrible to see her. She had loved him for years, it appeared."

"Did you know his name?"

186

"Yes, of course; he was a distant cousin, his name was Ashwin too."

"I'd no idea of that," Fleur exclaimed.

"Oh, it was hardly what you might call a relationship—three or four times removed or something like that. He hadn't a title either, just plain mister. Gerald was his Christian name."

"I met one of her cousins here. Did she ever speak of him—Anthony Ashwin?"

"Indeed she did. That's the one who was brought up with her like a brother, isn't it? I think she is annoyed with him, though, about something. Once or twice when she's been unhappy, she's said, 'It's Anthony's fault—he muddled things'; and another time she cried out, 'If only I hadn't listened to Anthony!' "

Fleur looked mystified.

"I wonder what happened? Poor Lady Cynthia, she must have been so lovely. It's cruel to see her as she is now."

"Oh, well, from all accounts she's had her fun all right," Nurse Thompson said with a giggle.

Fleur felt herself wince, there was something which jarred in the nurse's expression and voice.

"I wouldn't mind dying young myself if I'd had all that she has," Nurse Thompson went on. "Looks, title, money, and hundreds of men in love with her—what else could a woman want?"

"Her marriage wasn't a success," Fleur said gently.

"No, that's true enough, but are you surprised? Sir Norman seems a dry stick and I've seen photographs of Gerald Ashwin. He was good-looking all right. It was terrible for her his being killed like that on the very eve of their wedding."

"Yes, tragic."

"But do you know," Nurse Thompson said, sitting up and dropping her voice, "there's something queer about it. I can't tell you what because I don't know. But you can take it from me, Miss Garton, there's something behind all that."

"What do you mean?"

"Well, I can't exactly put it into words, and Lady Cynthia isn't the confiding sort; she's never said anything openly to me, but I've always felt in my bones that there's something that we don't know."

"What makes you think that?"

"I can't tell you. I wish I could. There, I've made you curious; I am myself, but I wouldn't mind betting you that there's a secret there all right."

Nurse Thompson got to her feet and stretched.

"Well, I can't keep my eyes open any longer. I'll be off to my downy couch. Good night."

"Good night, Nurse. I hope you sleep well."

Fleur was alone again, but she made no effort to pick up her book. Instead she sat staring into space, thinking.

The picture was by no means complete—there were so many pieces of the puzzle which would not fit in.

CHAPTER EIGHTEEN

It had been one of Mrs. Mitcham's bad days. She was querulous and disagreeable, and everyone who came in contact with her was at fault.

"She's desperately lonely," Fleur would remind herself.

When Mrs. Mitcham was difficult, when her voice was raised in anger and complaint, Fleur would think of her son, crouching in the corner of some squalid little room, trying to think, not of that hectoring tirade which fell from his mother's lips. But of the calm, grey peace of the Priory, of the black swans reflected on the silver water, of the glimmer of the setting sun rosy pink on the diamond-paned windows.

What happiness the Priory had been able to give him then! Fleur wondered if that secret solace had not meant a thousand times more to Norman than the actual fact of possession.

Often she would wonder how much the Priory still meant to him.

When Norman came back from his work, he always went up to see his mother, and Fleur, knowing how hard he was working tried to keep the old lady pleasant and good-humoured just before his arrival. Yet it was not always easy.

It was a sore subject with Mrs. Mitcham that she had not yet been allowed to see Cynthia and nearly every evening she tackled her son on this question, insisting that it was her right to welcome Cynthia to the Priory.

"She's too ill to have visitors," Norman would say briefly.

"There's no reason to count me as a visitor any more than Fleur," was Mrs. Mitcham's invariable retort, and it was difficult to find an answer.

This evening, mother and son had had more than their usual scrap over the subject of the visit to Cynthia and for once Norman's calm had been shattered.

"Do you think you are a good person to visit somebody who is very ill?" he asked his mother. "And at any rate, can't you leave the woman alone? She doesn't want to see you and the only reason you seek her is curiosity."

He walked out of Mrs. Mitcham's bedroom before she could reply, shutting the door behind him almost as noisily as Evans did when she was annoyed.

Fleur went down to dinner somewhat apprehensively. It was so unlike Norman to lose his temper with his mother that she felt something unusual must have occurred.

He was frowning as they walked into the dining-room, and dinner started in a silence which was all the more ominous because of late he had been more communicative.

Tonight he was as glum and morose as he had been when she first knew him, and finally Fleur could bear it no longer.

"Can't you tell me what's the matter?" she asked, striving to make both her voice and her question sound light. "I'm sure it's bad for our digestion to eat under this dark cloud of gloom."

"Yes, I'll tell you," Norman replied surprisingly. "Will you come down to the library after my mother's gone to bed?"

"I usually say good night to Lady Cynthia, but I'll come after that."

"You're so much in demand," he said, and she fancied there was the suspicion of a sneer in his voice, "that I never seem to be allowed my share of your company."

"That sounds most flattering, but actually you are the busy person, as you well know."

He passed his hand across his forehead.

"We've had a lot of trouble today. There was an accident in the works, rather a bad one. We've been very fortunate up to date so that I oughtn't to complain, but it's always disturbing although I think it was just chance."

"You mean that it could be sabotage?"

"There's always that possibility. Anyway, we shall know in about twenty-four hours after a thorough investigation has been made."

"No wonder he is worried," Fleur thought to herself, and noted that he poured himself out a stiff whisky and soda, an unusual action for he was practically a teetotaller.

She hurried Mrs. Mitcham off to bed that night and spent a shorter time than usual with Cynthia. For once she felt that Norman needed her more than they did. There was no one else in the house to whom he could talk.

His mother was still complaining plaintively of his behaviour; and Fleur knew that on the few and rare occasions on which he visited Cynthia they spoke shortly and conventionally to each other.

It was a cold evening and a fire was lit in the library. She found Norman walking up and down the room, a habit when he was unduly perturbed.

"I thought you were never coming."

"But I'm earlier than I expected to be," Fleur replied.

She moved across to the fire and sitting down on a low tapestry stool held her hands to the blaze. Norman stood looking down at her.

"Fleur," he said abruptly, "I can't go on like this."

She looked up at him with a startled expression on her face.

"What do you mean?"

"What I say," he answered roughly. "It's more than flesh and blood can stand. This situation is abnormal, no man can be expected to put up with it indefinitely."

"I don't understand," Fleur got to her feet.

"But of course you understand. You're a woman, aren't you? What do you expect me to feel? How do you expect me to stand it? This coming home every evening to find you entirely absorbed in the petty duties of the household, my mother whining and complaining and Cynthia lying there in her room—yet filling the house with her presence! I thought I'd escaped from all that, but apparently I was wrong."

He spoke with more emotion than Fleur had ever heard in his voice.

"You can't grudge her a bed here," she said quickly.

"Why not? Why should she come back and treat the house as if it were hers? It's mine, I tell you—she's no right to it; she's trying to make a fool of me once again; she's done it often enough before, and now you're helping here. You also are against me."

"That's not true," Fleur protested gently. "Lady Cynthia is a dying woman. The Priory means everything in the world to her, no one can understand that better than you can. And she's come home to die."

"She's being an unconscionable time about it."

Fleur looked at him in horror.

"How can you say such a thing!" she exclaimed.

In answer, he put out his hands and took her by the shoulders. It was the first time he had ever touched her. She felt herself stiffen.

"I say it," Norman replied, "because as long as Cynthia is in this house I realise I cannot approach you. She creates a barrier between us, a barrier which you believe is insurmountable. When I want a thing I fight for it, but Cynthia is using weapons against me which no normal man could combat. I want you, Fleur."

There was a passion in his voice that Fleur had never heard there before. She felt herself quiver and something in his eyes made her drop hers, feeling unable to face him, unwilling to read what was in his expression.

"I told you before that what you ask is impossible," she murmured.

She felt Norman's hands tighten on her shoulders until the strength of his fingers against her flesh was painful.

"Nothing is impossible for me. It never has been and I swear it never shall be. Nothing in the world shall prevent you from becoming my wife sooner or later."

Fleur made a sudden movement to be free and instantly he released her; but she felt as if she could not escape, could not evade him. She raised her eyes to his, her fingers interlaced one with the other.

"I didn't know you felt like this."

"You didn't think I loved you? Why else should I marry you?"

"I thought you wanted ... a mistress for the Priory," she stammered, hardly aware of what she said.

He laughed, a grim sound which echoed round the room and held no humour.

"The Priory—always the Priory! Yes, I offered you that as an inducement, as one might offer another woman diamonds; but do you think I was so blind, so stupid as not to want you for yourself? Perhaps it was just another impossible dream, and yet I felt that at last I had found a woman with whom I might have something in common, who might care for me apart from my possessions. Perhaps I was wrong."

He spoke bitterly, and Fleur, feeling suddenly guilty, remembered her own reaction to his proposal—her love for his house, and how she had shrunk from the thought of taking him with it.

"I don't understand," she said stupidly.

"Why should you?" he asked. "I meant to be patient, to go gently; I saw when I first spoke to you that I had frightened you, put you on the defensive, but I believed that time would play into my hands. Instead, Cynthia has come here to make things not only more difficult, but definitely unbearable.

"Fleur, I need you. Marry me now and at once. Let's go away a little while from these ill women. They can have nurses and doctors to attend to them, everything in the world they require but you."

"Please ... please, Sir Norman."

She put out her hands in front of her as if she would ward him off, although he made no movement towards her.

She felt she was being overpowered, captured and held against her will; the force of his determination was so strong that she was afraid ... afraid of being coerced ... afraid of being unable to resist this stronger, dominating will.

"That is no answer," he said, grimly.

He stood there looking at her, and suddenly she felt she could bear the tension no longer. Blindly she turned towards the door.

As if he had anticipated her move, Norman barred the way.

"Don't go until you have answered me."

"But I can't! Don't you understand I can't!" Fleur cried wildly. "I'd no idea that you felt like this about me. Let me go now ... let me think about it, I can't decide a question such as this in a second."

"Why not?"

Again he was not actually touching her, but she felt as if he held her encompassed about with bands of steel.

"It's impossible, you must see that."

"I've already given you the answer to that," he said.

Then, as she looked up into his face, her eyes wide and worried, her mouth trembling a little with distress, he put out his arms and drew her close to him.

She gave a convulsive movement as if she would struggle; then as he made no effort to kiss her, but only held her there with her head against his shoulder, she was still.

"Can't you think of me just as a man who needs you, Fleur?" Norman was saying in a voice unbelievably tender, unrecognisably gentle. "I've always been lonely, but I never knew how lonely until you came here. It's been agony to let you go away every evening after dinner, to know that I must stay here reading or thinking while you were moving about upstairs. I want to see you, I want to watch you, I want to hear what you think, to understand what you are feeling. Perhaps I'm a fool to say these things to you, perhaps you'll laugh about it with your friends.

"No, no," he said as Fleur gave an exclamation; "don't bother to reply. I know you wouldn't do that, you're different, but it has been done to me in the past. Oh, my dear, can't either of us ever forget our past?"

He held her close for another moment, then quite suddenly he released her. While she stood trembling and irresolute, he walked away to stand looking down at the fire, his back towards her, his head bent.

"You'd better go now," he said, gruffly. "I have a feeling that I've made a fool of myself again."

She longed to say something, to bring some comfort to him, but she could only stare at his back, feeling the total inadequacy of any words she might utter.

Then, as he did not move or speak again, she went quietly from the room, closing the door behind her.

CHAPTER NINETEEN

Fleur had felt desperately shy at the thought of meeting Sir Norman again.

But she need not have worried, need not have spent agonising hours wondering what she would say to him, planning how she could reopen the subject of their marriage and make him understand once and for all it was impossible.

Events prevented them from seeing each other alone. To begin with, two important officials from the Ministry of Aircraft Production arrived to stay unexpectedly and absorbed every moment of Norman's time.

Then Cynthia became worse, doctors came and went, specialists from London had to be given meals at odd hours, nurses fluttered about the house, looking in their starched aprons and white caps like agitated doves.

Fleur found herself run off her feet, especially as Mrs. Mitcham feeling herself outside the general flurry and excitement, tried to assert her right to monopolise most of her companion's time.

In the midst of it all, Fleur, taking up a local paper which had been laid in the hall with the other newspapers, saw Jack's face staring at her from a wedding group.

For a moment she waited, every muscle in her body tense in anticipation of pain; then she relaxed, realising that incredibly and without warning, his power to hurt her had gone. He belonged to the past.

She could not remember now how long it was since she had cried out in her longing for him, how many weeks, or, indeed, months since she had gone to sleep murmuring his name, holding out her empty, aching arms to the darkness.

Quite calmly and without unhappiness she could look down at his smiling face as he stood in the arched doorway of a church with Nancy on his arm.

The photograph was headed: "A Picturesque Wedding of Local Interest", and Fleur could see behind the bride and bridegroom, just emerging from the shadows the compressed lips and thin, sharp features of Mrs. Reynolds.

Quite suddenly she knew that she was glad she had escaped that smug respectability, that life of inevitable mediocrity.

And Jack? What did she feel about Jack, she asked herself, and knew that in losing Jack she had escaped from passion.

"I'm free!" Fleur cried aloud that night as she went to bed, and wondered why people ever sought for love, believing it could bring them a happiness greater than that of being self-sufficient.

The thought of Sir Norman came to her instantly and she sighed for him.

"But he doesn't love me," she reassured herself, "as I have loved Lucien and Jack. His is a different type of love."

As she formulated the idea, however, she wondered if it were true. Was love in the moment of its happening ever different? Wasn't it always the same—moments of springing, pulsating ecstasy and moments of utter despondency and despair?

She felt uneasy about Sir Norman. Were he really to love her in such a way, it would be in her power to make him unhappy, to add to the suffering he had already experienced in his life.

Women had been unlucky for him—his mother, Cynthia, and now perhaps, herself.

"Poor Sir Norman!" She found herself pitying him, and then was half-inclined to laugh at the idea. Who in their senses would pity Sir Norman Mitcham, the millionaire, the most powerful man in industry, one of the key men of the country's war effort?

Uneasily, Fleur turned and twisted in her bed. How could she help Sir Norman, how could she bring him some sort of happiness apart, of course, from the sacrifice of herself?

Still thinking of Sir Norman, Fleur must have fallen into an uneasy slumber, for when there came a sharp rap on her door she awoke with a start.

"Miss Garton, can I come in?"

Cynthia's night nurse put her head round the door.

"Yes, of course," Fleur replied, sitting up in bed and switching on the light. "What's the matter? Is anything wrong?"

"I'm sorry to wake you up but Lady Cynthia insisted. She wants to see you."

"At this hour!" Fleur exclaimed.

She looked at her little travelling clock, seeing that the hands pointed to twenty past two.

"I tried to dissuade her," the nurse said, apologetically, "but she was so insistent that I had to agree. As you know, she's had a bad day and the great thing is not to agitate her."

"I'll come at once," Fleur said, getting out of bed. "Have you any idea what she wants?"

"She won't tell me. Just said she wanted to see you and insisted on my giving her what she calls her 'buckup' drops. She's not supposed to have them except in an emergency, but there—if you're as bad as she is, it doesn't seem to me to matter much what you do. Better have what you can while you can get it is my motto in such circumstances. Shall I tell her you're coming?"

"Yes, please; I won't be a moment."

Fleur had wrapped herself in her dressing-gown and

now she sat for a moment before her looking-glass, combing her hair and giving a touch of powder to her nose, then she hurried along the passage to Cynthia's room.

A fire was lit and there was an exquisite fragrance of hothouse flowers, carnations and lilies, arranged in big bowls on the dressing-table.

"Come in, Fleur," Cynthia said. "Are you furious with me for sending for you?"

"Of course not. You know I'm always ready to come if you want me."

She felt with a sudden pang of pity that Cynthia looked very wan. Her face had wasted in the last few weeks, her eyes were now abnormally large and dark.

Her voice was weak, too, and Fleur, knowing it was an effort for her to speak, drew near to the bed, drawing up a chair so that she was only a few feet away.

"Are we alone?" Cynthia asked.

The night nurse heard the question and nodding to Fleur, went out of the room, shutting the door quietly behind her.

"Yes, we are quite alone."

"Then, listen," Cynthia started. "I want you to help me, Fleur. Will you promise to help me?"

"But of course I will," Fleur said. "If there's anything I can do, you know I'd be happy to do it for you."

"You don't know yet what I'm going to ask you, but you're the only person who can help me, I realise that."

"Then tell me what it is."

Cynthia hesitated a moment, then looking at Fleur searchingly she said:

"You know I'm dying. No, don't contradict me. I know it only too well. I've watched the faces of the doctors and the nurses and I know that they've given me up. They've tried everything possible and they've failed. It's only a question of weeks, perhaps days, and I don't mind, you know that, I've had my life and I'm content to go; but there's just one thing I want, one small thing before I die."

"What's that?"

"To see my son," Cynthia said.

Then she continued as Fleur made an involuntary movement of surprise, "That's what I've got to tell you about and that is why you—and only you—can help me."

Her voice weakened, almost failed. She pointed to a bottle by her bedside.

"Give me three drops in a little water."

"Hadn't I better ask nurse?"

"No, it's all rght."

Fleur did as she was told. After she had drunk the mixture Cynthia's voice was stronger again. She lay back against her pillows and put out her hand.

"Give me your hand, Fleur. Come very close to me. I've got a long story to tell you, I don't want to fail before it is finished."

Fleur obeyed her. Cynthia's hand was thin and small and her skin was hot and dry, yet it seemed to Fleur that she clung to her with a surprising strength. Through the physical contact she sensed the tremendous determination which lay behind the effort Cynthia was making.

"You know why I married Norman," Cynthia began. "We've spoken of that before, but what you don't know and what Norman didn't know either was that when I married him I was desperately in love with someone else—with Gerald, my cousin whom I'd known ever since I was a child.

"I think I'd always loved Gerald and he me; we'd grown up knowing it, knowing, too, that we belonged to each other utterly and completely. But he was in the Army and, of course, he had no money—none of the Ashwins have.

"Just before my father died, Gerald was sent to India. We said good-bye, not feeling it was anything of tremendous importance that we should be separated for a year or so.

"When Father died and the Priory came to me, Gerald was not there to help me through the ghastly shock of discovering the state of our finances. My father had let things drift, taxes were unpaid, debts had accumulated, and combined with all this we had to find an almost staggering sum in death duties.

"I was desperate and there was no one to whom I could turn except Anthony—Anthony who had always been like a brother, who had lived at the Priory, who had grown up loving it nearly as much as I did.

"It was Anthony who discovered that the one thing Norman wanted more than anything else in the world was to own this house.

"I tried to write to Gerald to tell him what was happening, but letters are a hopeless medium of expression and I was never good at putting my feelings on paper. I had to do something and do it quickly. You know the choice I made.

"A year after I had married Norman, Gerald came home. I suppose, looking back on things, I behaved about as badly to Norman as any woman could, and yet I wonder if I can make you understand that I never felt married to him.

"He never seemed real, somehow, this husband of mine with whom I had no thought in common, no interests save one—the house we lived in and which now belonged to him.

"And for that I hated him. It sounds ridiculous now, put into words; but I resented him, I resented his money, and I loathed him for being a usurper, for sitting in the place which I believed by rights should have been Gerald's.

"We behaved abominably, Anthony and I. When I think of it now, I'm ashamed. We filled the house with gay and amusing people, the people who had always loved us and who lived the sort of life we knew and understood. They had nothing in common with Norman. They sneered at him, sneered at his lack of breeding and his unlimited wealth, sneered because inwardly they were envious.

"I stood by and let them do it because I was envious

too, envious of Norman's position in my life, envious and jealous that he should have what ought to have been Gerald's."

Cynthia was overcome by a fit of coughing. The nurse came hurrying through the door. When the paroxysm had passed she lay back on the pillow with her eyes closed.

"Now you must go to sleep," the nurse insisted; but Cynthia waved her away.

"I haven't finished," she said. "I've got to go on."

The nurse would have protested, but Cynthia's determination drove her from the room. Fleur drew near again to the bedside, Cynthia's hand reached out to clasp hers.

Again that low, intense voice took up the story.

"You can guess what happened," Cynthia whispered. "I was never good at resisting temptation, besides, I felt no loyalty to Norman. How could I belong to him—that silent stranger whose only reason for being in my life at all was that he had bought me and the Priory.

"I spent week-ends in London with Gerald; I used to creep out at night and motor across country to a little cottage he rented about ten miles from here. He gave up coming to the house, he wouldn't betray a man under his own roof even while I could never feel that the Priory was Norman's, but mine—mine and my family's.

"After a time, Norman grew suspicious. It was not surprising. He had little home life. What there was of it was noisy and I imagine unattractive. The house was always full of people, and Norman seldom saw me alone.

"At last one night he came to my room very late. I told him I wanted to sleep. We had been dancing until long after midnight, and the night before I had been with Gerald, although he did not know that, and had not returned until dawn had broken. For the first and only time in our married life Norman tried to assert his rights.

202

" 'I want a wife,' he told me, 'I want a mother for my children.'

"I laughed then. Oh, it was cruel of me, but I loved Gerald; I was crazily, madly in love with him; the idea of Norman supplanting such an affection in my heart was merely ridiculous.

"I picked up a little doll—it was a toy which had come out of one of the crackers at Christmas and which I had kept on my mantelpiece.

" 'This is the only child you and I are likely to have,' I said, and without a word he took it from me and left the room.

"I remember feeling a little hysterical after he had gone. Inwardly I was ashamed of myself, outwardly I was defiant. It was just a few weeks later that I realised that I was going to have Gerald's child.

"I thought over the situation very carefully. It seemed to me then that I grew up suddenly overnight. I saw what I had done, the mistakes I had made, and yet there seemed to me one hope, a strange one perhaps, but egotistically I thought of it only from my own viewpoint—the hope that Norman might accept my child."

"Unknowingly?" Fleur asked.

"No, of course not," Cynthia replied. "We hadn't lived together since Gerald's return from India. No, I should have to tell him, but I thought that he might in his generosity let me bring up the child to inherit the Priory. Here was the heir that he'd wanted, and to me there was a supreme satisfaction in knowing that my baby was an Ashwin.

"The family could continue here in the house that had always been theirs. I suppose it all sounds fantastic to you; but when I thought of it then, it seemed to me so sensible. I talked it over with Gerald and with Anthony.

"They were dubious, but I swayed them round to my opinion. I believed that I could do anything with Norman—I was certain I could. After all, he had loved me for many years, almost since he had first come to the Priory as the boot-boy.

" 'Leave it to me,' I said. 'Norman will agree what I suggest.'

"I suppose until that moment I'd never been denied anything that I wanted very much in life.

"I told Norman. The house was, as usual, filled with people and I went to his room after everyone had gone to bed. He was surprised to see me, but courteous and polite, as if I was a stranger asking his advice in the office.

"I told him frankly the condition I was in and I made my suggestion that he should accept the child, which was legally his. He said nothing at first and I think I told him how grateful I would be and how much it would mean to me in the future.

"And then, when I had said all there was to say, I stopped talking; and as my voice ceased, I realized for the first time that I was afraid ... afraid of Norman ... afraid of what he would say and do.

"He stood looking at me without speaking and I think that for the first time since I'd married him I realised that he was a definite person to be contended with, not just a boy who had cleaned the boots or a common young man whom I had patronised and made blush by my kindness.

"He was not the older man who had stammered an almost incoherent proposal of marriage which I had decided to accept before he even made it; he was not the quiet unobtrusive husband whom no one had noticed about the place and whom I'd forgotten completely in the wonder and happiness of my love for Gerald.

"He was someone relentless, cruel and resolute, whom I could not sway, could not alter.

"He turned away, and then from a drawer in the table he fetched the idiotic little doll I had given him. He recalled my taunting words, he repeated them to me bitterly and cruelly. I knew then that I had sinned against him beyond redemption, that nothing I could do or say would ever erase the past.

"He told me coldly and dispassionately that when my child was born he would make a public announcement to the effect that it was not his, he would leave it not one penny of his money nor should it ever inherit the Priory.

"I cried, I pleaded, I persisted; but I knew it was useless. Norman had his revenge then for all I had ever made him suffer.

"There was only one thing I could do—go away. I went out to Kenya; I arranged with an aunt of mine by marriage, the wife of my father's brother, that she and her husband would take the child as soon as it was born.

"She was an attractive woman, lovable and sweet, and only ten years older than myself. It had been a bitter disappointment to her and her husband that they had never been able to have any children.

"My son was born in their house; a few of my intimate friends knew about it, but no one else; there was no publicity, no talk. They adopted the boy who took their name—which, indeed, was his own—Gerry Ashwin.

"As soon as I was well again, I came back to England to see Norman. I begged him to divorce me. Gerald and I were determined that no stigma should be attached to our child, but we felt that if we were married it would be easy to have him to live with us and in time people would forget that there was anything mysterious about his birth.

"Norman refused me my divorce. I then knew I had lost everything. Gerald was anxious not to give up his Regiment and it was difficult for us to see each other for any length of time. We would have a week or so together when he could get leave, then months and months of agonising loneliness.

"I had money, that was all—the money which Norman had given me in exchange for the Priory. I think I realised then how utterly worthless money is when it can buy none of the things you really need in life.

"At last Norman relented. It was only after I had been to a clever and unscrupulous lawyer who said that he thought I might bring an action in which I could prove that I had never been legally entitled to break the entail of the Priory.

"I think we should have lost the case, but Norman preferred to give me the divorce I wanted rather than allow his possession to be called in question. The Priory was the only thing he had wanted above all others and it gave him, I suppose, a great satisfaction to be the unquestioned owner of the house where he had once been its most unimportant servant.

"He divorced me and the day after the decree was made absolute, I had arranged to marry Gerald. You know what happened—you know how he was killed.

"I think then that I died with him. I have cared for nothing since, I've only been impatient with this illness which has taken so long to deliver me from life.

"Death has no fears for me—why should it?—for if there is an eternity, Gerald will be there waiting for me. We have never been parted so long as this before.

"But before I go to him, I want to see his son. Gerry doesn't know that I'm his mother. We've never told him and there's no reason for him to know it now.

"But if you would persuade Norman to let him come here . . . so that I can see him for the last time, touch his soft curly head . . . kiss him just once . . . can you persuade Norman? . . . can you?"

Cynthia's voice broke and Fleur was conscious that the tears were running down her own face.

"I'll try . . . of course I'll try," she murmured.

"What a mess I've made of things!" Cynthia said through lips that tried to smile; "and yet, somehow, it doesn't seem to matter. Gerald will put things right for me, but I want to tell him that all's well with our son. Will you send for little Gerry, Fleur?"

CHAPTER TWENTY

Fleur, peeping from behind the drawn blind, watched the funeral procession winding slowly like a black snake down the drive towards Greystone church.

The coffin was covered with flowers, and most of the mourners carried a wreath of some sort, yet even so, the whole impression of the procession was one of morbid gloom.

The procession was turning, leaving the drive to take a side walk across the fields to the church. Now she could see them clearly—the coffin drawn along by the men of the household, old Barham walking first, his face, Fleur knew, creased and wrinkled in sorrow.

Immediately behind the coffin came Sir Norman—Norman and Anthony, side by side. Fleur had wondered up to the last moment whether Norman would go to the funeral; it was a difficult position for him to be in.

There was no precedent for what was correct in such abnormal circumstances, but Anthony had taken it for granted that he would be there and to Fleur's surprise, Norman had acquiesced agreeably to all that was expected of him.

Behind Norman were Colonel Ashwin, his wife and Gerry. Fleur could see the little boy quite clearly, walking straight and erect, his head held high, his shoulders back.

From the moment Gerry had entered the house Fleur had found herself liking the child more than was reasonable for someone who meant so little in her life.

He was everything, she thought, that one would like one's own son to be; handsome, good-mannered and interesting, yet not precocious, talkative without being in any way self-opinionated.

It was easy to see how Colonel and Mrs. Ashwin adored him and he them. Fleur had wondered if in the past Cynthia must not often have felt a pang of envy or jealousy when she saw the affection exchanged between her own son and those who had adopted him.

And in the first few minutes after meeting Gerry she could understand how much Cynthia had wanted to see him again, how she could not relinquish her hold on life without one last look at the son she had borne—a son who must remind her in every movement, in every gesture, of the man she had loved and lost.

It seemed as if that last farewell brought her comfort and gave her the last mortal thing she desired, for two days after Gerry had come to the house, Cynthia had died.

She had passed away peacefully and it was impossible to mourn her; there was so little she had cared for in this world and so much waiting for her on the other side.

She had died in her sleep and there was a smile on her lips as if she was well content.

It was Gerry who made things easy for them all, who put death into its right perspective, who swept the tears from their eyes. Even that dreaded moment when he had arrived at the Priory and must meet Sir Norman had passed off easily.

Fleur had shrunk from it and yet she need not have been afraid. Colonel and Mrs. Ashwin had arrived while Norman was still at the factory. When he returned, unexpectedly early, Fleur and Gerry were alone in the hall.

They had just come in from the garden and Gerry

was talking animatedly of the ponies they had seen down by the stables. He broke off his conversation as Sir Norman walked through the front door drawing off his gloves.

For a moment Fleur felt at a loss. She sensed Sir Norman's instinctive reaction to Gerry's presence, she felt the antagonism which vibrated from him; then she heard her own voice, breathless and rather frightened, saying:

"This is Gerry, Sir Norman."

Gerry held out his hand.

"How do you do, Sir?"

For a moment Fleur thought that Norman was going to ignore the boy; then he took the hand he was offered, murmured something almost inaudible and turned towards the library.

"Who is that?" Gerry asked in a whisper.

"Sir Norman Mitcham," Fleur replied. "This is his house, you know."

"I thought it was," Gerry said. Then, speeding across the widening space between Norman and himself, he said: "I say, Sir, do you think that while I'm here you could take me round the factory?"

Norman stopped abruptly; he was frowning, Fleur noticed, and she fancied that his fingers were clenched.

"Why?" He asked the question curtly, the monosyllable sounding almost unnaturally loud.

Gerry looked up at him eagerly.

"I love cars. My father told me you made the Mitchams—we've got one, you know, and sometimes Jenkins—that's our chauffeur—lets me hold the wheel. I've watched him mend it, too. I'm going to learn all about engines and when I'm grown up I mean to be a mechanic."

"Oh, you do, do you?" Norman said.

It was impossible not to respond to the boy's excitement, it was so obvious that he already had for Norman a sort of hero-worship.

Quite suddenly Fleur had felt the tears pricking her

eyes. The whole moment was so poignant and at the same time so infinitely pitiable.

Yes, Gerry would have his wish, she thought now as she watched them moving across the field. Norman had promised him all he asked for, it would have taken a far harder man than Norman to resist Gerry.

He had, it appeared, a passion for engines. Machinery of all sorts fascinated him, but especially anything to do with cars or aeroplanes.

That Norman should be the actual inventor and creator of such things gave him, in Gerry's mind, an almost godlike omnipotence.

"When is Sir Norman coming home?" he would ask, not once, but a dozen times before luncheon and again in the evening. "There's something I want to ask him."

As soon as there came the sound of Norman's car outside, he would tear down the front steps, rush to greet him and shower forth innumerable questions to which he believed only Norman could give him the correct answers.

If only he had been Norman's son, Fleur found herself thinking over and over again, and guessed that in his innermost heart Norman thought the same.

It was funny now, after living for a week under the same roof as Norman and Gerry, to realise how much she had dreaded their meeting and how needless her fears and anticipations had been.

But she told herself that no one had ever had a more difficult task to attempt than that which Cynthia had pleaded with her to undertake.

When she had left Cynthia's room that night after she had heard the true story of Norman's miserable misfit marriage, she had lain awake until dawn wondering how she could possibly tackle him on the subject of Gerry.

It had taken all her courage and all her resolution to go to him the next morning.

She knew that she herself was trembling as she faced him across the big desk in the library. Norman had been telephoning when she came into the room and she had sat down, waiting for him to finish. Then as he replaced the receiver, he had smiled at her.

"What can I do for you, Fleur?"

It was the first time they had been alone since that night when his reserve had fallen and he had told her how much he needed her, had begged her to become his wife. Fleur felt herself flushing, the warm colour rising in her cheeks.

"Norman," she said, "I've got something difficult to ask you."

It was the first time she had addressed him familiarly; it was involuntary and she only realised what she had said when she saw the pleased response in his eyes.

"Well, what is it?" he asked. "Don't look so frightened, my dear."

"I am frightened," Fleur confessed, and knew that her heart was thumping.

He got up from his chair and walked round the desk to stand close to her. He put out his hand and laid it on hers.

"What is it?" he asked, and his voice was grave.

Instinctively Fleur's fingers closed on his, she held on to him tightly, firmly, as if she dare not let him go while she told him what she wanted.

She looked away from him as she spoke, her eyes resting on the blotter which lay closed on Norman's desk—an ornate piece of leatherwork bearing the Ashwin coat-of-arms.

Then he made a movement as if he would release his hand.

"Please, Norman . . . please?"

Fleur felt that she was pleading with him for her very life. She turned to face him and saw what she had feared—his face white and drawn, an expression which told her ominously that she must expect a refusal.

"You don't understand what you ask." Norman had spoken at last, his voice rough and raw.

"But I do understand—of course I do . . . and yet

211

can't you see that it doesn't really matter to you now? Cynthia belongs to your past. You can be generous, magnanimous, because she is powerless to hurt you unless you let her."

"What do you mean?"

"That Cynthia's power over you rests only in the memory of your own injuries. You loved her once. Do you still love her? I do not think that you do—therefore she cannot hurt you. Nothing she can do can really give you pain save that which you deliberately invoke mentally in memories from the past. Gerry is her son—you have already made her suffer for having him. I think that she has been punished enough."

"I'm glad you think so." Norman spoke bitterly.

Fleur released his hand at last and got to her feet.

"Even if she has not," she said quietly, "it is not for you to play God—surely you recognise that? The boy is hers—he is also an Ashwin; they both belong here, Norman, you can't refuse this last request."

There was an ominous pause and then, so unexpectedly that Fleur was left with nothing to say, Norman answered: "Very well, then, I can't refuse it."

"You mean ... ?"

"What I have said. Please make all the necessary arrangements."

He turned away from her deliberately, and Fleur knew herself dismissed, and in that moment swiftly the thought came to her—"Now I have lost him."

Later that evening, after a long day and when she was at last alone, she was certain that her instinct had been right—Norman had finished with her. Strangely enough, the idea was disconcerting and upsetting.

Immediately after the funeral the majority of the guests would be leaving. Cars had already been ordered to take them to the station, and the following afternoon Colonel and Mrs. Ashwin and Gerry would be returning home too.

The house would revert to normal, and yet Fleur wondered if it would be possible ever to find a level of normality again after all that they had been through, after all she had known and felt when Cynthia was with them.

Quite suddenly she knew she could not stay. Norman no longer cared for her, she was certain of that, and her own feelings about Norman were too chaotic, too much in a state of flux for her to be certain what they were.

Of one thing, however, she was sure, she could not bear the icy recrimination of his voice and the feeling that he was accusing her, silently, but nevertheless vehemently, of betraying his affection even as the other women in his life had betrayed it.

"I must go away," Fleur thought, and realised that now was her opportunity.

The old lady was asleep now and Fleur decided that she would leave her a note. She would leave one also for Norman.

She took one last look at the procession of mourners passing through the fields; the coffin had now reached the gate leading into the churchyard; she could see the parson in his white surplice, waiting in the shadows of the porch.

She turned away and went towards her writing table. The light was dim and she switched on a lamp.

She picked up her pen, drew a sheet of notepaper into position, and then quite suddenly and without warning, the tears came streaming into her eyes.

She was not certain why she cried, she only knew that the future seemed dark and comfortless and she was afraid for herself.

CHAPTER TWENTY-ONE

Fleur sat despondently on her bed in a narrow, unattractive room whose windows looked out over the roofs of Kensington.

She had come to this old-fashioned, second-rate hotel because she remembered it as being cheap; a secretary of her father's had stayed there for many years and Fleur had often visited her, carrying manuscripts which were ready for typing or spending the afternoon during her holidays from school.

But she had never known until now how depressing such places could be when one actually had to live in them.

There was the smell of cooking which always pervaded the stairs; the stair-carpet which was threadbare and still floridly ugly; the banisters sadly in need of polish. The bathrooms opening off the landings, which with their frosted windows, stained enamel and linoleum from which the patterns had been worn away made the idea of cleanliness distinctly uninviting.

There was, too, something inexpressibly dismal about the guests in the hotel.

They were mostly old spinsters who had lived there for years, striving to make a home in the shabby, impersonal bedrooms and in the pretentious drabness of reception rooms which, like those who inhabited them, had once seen better days.

"Shall I become like these women?" Fleur wondered.

She looked at them with their endless knitting, their rheumaticky fingers, their array of glasses for reading and sewing, and their rigidly-adhered-to habit of sitting in the same place at the same time, day after day, evening after evening.

Listening to their querulous voices rising and falling in the lounge, she was seized with a nostalgia for the Priory which shook her as if she found herself caught in a tempest at sea.

And yet, she asked herself, was it really the Priory for which she longed, was it not for the people she knew there?

She knew then that she missed Norman more than she would have believed possible.

As the realisation came to her, flooding her consciousness, swamping her with its implication, she had risen from her chair in the lounge and gone upstairs to her own bedroom to stand at the window.

She looked out at the sky from which the sun was fading, at the smoke rising from a hundred chimneys, dark and dingy above the grey, weatherbeaten roofs.

She could imagine the loveliness of the Priory at this hour of the evening, the reflection of cloud and crimson sunset on the lake, the song of the birds as they went to roost, the strange calm and peace which would descend on the house and gardens as if some divine hand was laid on it in blessing.

"Why did I leave?" Fleur asked herself, and knew the answer—that she could not stay, feeling that she had failed Norman, and had lost both his respect and affection.

Strange how cowardly she was where he was concerned; and yet she wondered if the truth was not that instinctively within herself she realised that he had the power to hurt her, to wound her perhaps more deeply than anyone else had ever been able to before.

It seemed to her that the strange emotion which possessed her when she thought of Norman struck down into the very depths of her being, and was too overpowering and too tremendous ever to be thought of in the same category as the love she had known in the past.

Her love for Lucien and Jack—what had it been? The excitement and thrill of knowing oneself beloved, the seeking of youth for youth, a desire as easy as that of a bee sipping honey from the flower.

But with Norman it was different.

This was the solidarity of a tree growing slowly but surely to strength and magnificence, roots delving underground so that they held steadfast against gale and tempest, against affliction and pain—roots which could not be torn up or destroyed for a whim.

"Oh, God," Fleur prayed, "what am I to do now?"

She had spent the three days since she came to London looking for a job.

The Labour Exchange had been helpful, but at the same time it was difficult to find a place where she could do a useful job of work until she was really strong. She had visited a doctor who told her that she must take things easy for at least another six weeks.

"Otherwise I will not be responsible for what may happen," he said. "Your heart is still slightly affected. It would be best, of course, for you to be in the country."

"I'd rather be in London," Fleur had replied, but gave no reason for being contrary.

He would not have understood that she felt it would be easier in an environment of complete contrast to forget what she had left behind, to erase yet another part of her life which must now belong only to the past.

Today she had heard of a position which sounded as though it might suit her.

It was in a solicitor's office. It would be dull work, monotonous work, but it was within her capabilities as she was required to do neither shorthand nor typing in which she was unskilled.

She had been given an appointment for the next day, but she felt dully that the matter was already settled.

She saw the future lving ahead of her like a long, dark tunnel without a glimpse of light within it.

"I suppose I'm a fool!" Fleur said aloud to herself.

She wondered how many other women would have been so stupid as to relinquish a post at the Priory, to leave without learning the truth finally and conclusively from Norman's own lips.

Yet there had been no misunderstanding the icy coldness of his voice as he had dismissed her from the study to make the plans for Gerry's arrival; there had been no mistaking the way he had avoided coming in contact with her while the funeral was taking place.

Besides, ridiculously, but inescapably, Fleur felt that Gerry stood between her and Norman. It might be an absurd idea, but it was nevertheless insistent in her mind that Norman was usurping Gerry's rightful place and position.

Dear little Gerry! Fleur had the warmest and most affectionate thoughts for Cynthia's son.

It was nice to think that he would always be happy and protected in the home that his mother had chosen for him, that he would grow up to manhood unaware of the dark tragedies and passions which had attended his birth.

Cynthia was in the hands of God; Gerry provided for ... that only left Norman, and suddenly Fleur covered her face with her hands and sat down on the bed.

Wildly she found herself praying for Norman's future, that somehow he might find peace and rest from the unhappiness he carried within himself ...

How long she sat there she did not know, but when she took her hands from her face it was growing dark.

She made no effort to undress, but sat on in the evening twilight watching the stars come out one by one in the deepening sky.

"Tomorrow," she thought, "I will leave here. I can bear this place no longer. I will find somewhere gayer,

217

more modern—there must be hotels or boarding-houses which are not so dreary."

She had written to her bank and asked them to transfer her account from Seaford to London. She was thankful that she had quite a considerable balance standing to her credit, for she had left the Priory without her wages, taking, she felt, little more than she had brought to it.

Indeed, if her time there was measured in other terms than money, she had given much more than she had received—her loyalty, her affection, and at last her love . . .

It was as if the house swept aside all superficiality from those who lived in it and drew out the most fundamental emotions, not always happy ones, but invariably those that were most intense.

Fleur, closing her eyes wearily, wondered if, like Cynthia, Norman and so many others, she too was to be haunted by the Priory for the rest of her life. Was it a vampire in the way it battened upon human beings, drawing from their very life-blood?

Suddenly there was a knock at the door.

For a moment Fleur could hardly collect herself to answer—she had been far away, lost in thought and in recollection—then she got up off the bed and opened the door.

A little maid stood there, merely a child who looked strangely overdressed in her uniform with its perky frilled cap and fancy apron.

"Someone to see you, miss."

"To see me!" Fleur exclaimed. "Who is it, and surely it's very late?"

"It's a gentleman, and it's nearly eleven o'clock, miss. I was just going to bed myself and the old ladies have gone ages ago. You'll have the lounge to yourselves."

Without a word Fleur started slowly to descend the stairs. As she went, she knew that her heart was beating quickly and she felt an eager, springing hope within herself which would not be denied.

"It's ridiculous!" she thought. "It couldn't be!"

And yet she prayed that it might be so.

She opened the door of the lounge. Norman was standing at the far end before the empty fireplace.

Her first impression was that he looked bigger and broader; he seemed to dominate the shabby room with its oddly assorted armchairs, its occasional tables, its oriental china vases containing pampas grass.

"I have never known him look so distinguished," Fleur thought.

Then she understood. She had never before seen Norman without the Priory as a background. Away from that he had an importance of his own, for his character and his personality were not swamped and distorted by the comparison.

She walked slowly across the room. He made no movement towards her and said nothing until she was close beside him, then abruptly, in the manner which was so characteristic of him, he asked:

"Why did you run away?"

Fleur was conscious that her pulses were racing and that her mouth was dry. She parried his question with one of her own.

"How did you find me?"

"I telephoned your bank early this morning. They told me that they had heard from you and I came to London as soon as I could get away."

"I'm sorry I've put you to so much ... trouble."

"You haven't answered my question. Why did you run away?"

"I don't think I can answer that."

Fleur looked down as she spoke, unable to meet his eyes.

"Why not?"

She almost laughed, it was such joy to endure his sharp questioning again.

"I can't ... explain."

Norman's arms reached out and he took her by the shoulders. She remembered that night at the Priory when he had done the same thing and knew that now her reaction was so very different. For she felt neither shrinking nor fear, but rather an inner gladness, a joy which was inexpressible.

"Why not?" Norman repeated again.

She raised her face and looked into his. What she saw there in his eyes and in the queer, tender curve of his lips held her spellbound.

"Was it because of the boy?" Norman asked, and still she could not reply, so that without waiting for her answer he went on: "I felt it might be, and after you'd gone I began to think of many things. I remembered what you said about Cynthia's power to hurt me having gone; I remembered too how you alleged that she and Gerry belonged to the Priory. You were right, Fleur! It's taken a long time to make me understand what you meant, but I do understand at last. Are you glad?"

She tried to force the words of affirmation between her lips, but somehow she could say nothing, only stand there, trembling.

She could feel his hands, was aware of the hardness of them through the thin chiffon sleeves of her dress, and she was acutely conscious of his nearness—of those dark eyes staring down at her, of those firm lips so near to her own.

"There are many things I want to tell you," Norman was saying, "and many things I want to hear, but I will say this first. The reason why I could not come to London in search of you on an earlier train today was because I had certain business to attend to. That business concerned you."

"Concerned . . . me!" Fleur echoed.

"Very intimately, and I can't help wondering a little anxiously how much it will affect our future, Fleur—yours and mine."

She made a little movement at the words and instantly, as if he suspected that she wished to be free, he released her. Then, standing quite near, but not touching her, he said:

"Today I have made over the Priory and all its contents in trust for Cynthia's son, Gerry Ashwin. But until the war is ended I shall stay there and the rest of the house will be used as a convalescent home for men in the R.A.F."

Fleur gave an incoherent exclamation and he went on:

"It was you who made me see clearly and unmistakably that I could never really own the Priory. I dreamt of doing so, but it was the dream of a common boy from the back streets who presumed to ape his betters."

"No, no, you mustn't think that!" Fleur could speak now.

She moved swiftly forward to put her hand protectingly against his arm as if she would have him from the bitterness of his own thoughts.

"Then for what reason am I so unworthy?"

"Never, never that!" Fleur expostulated. "You are worthy of so much that is fine and good. But don't you understand, don't you see that the Priory swamps you, belittles you—cripples you, if you like?

"Because, beautiful and marvellous as it is, the Priory is concerned only with what is past, never with what is to come. It is static. It is exquisite—a jewel, but it has attained perfection, it can never improve, can never blossom or grow.

"Your whole life has been one of going forward, of service to others . . . but there is much more for you to do, much more for you to attain.

"Can't you realise that by saddling yourself with the Priory, by cramping your progress—a meteoric one— with the laboured accumulation of centuries, you put everything out of perspective? It's like looking at you down the wrong end of a telescope.

"Now you are free, untrammelled, unburdened! And I'm glad . . . terribly glad . . . not only for Gerry's sake but for yours. Oh, Norman, so very . . . glad!"

He looked down at her eager, flushed face and shin-

221

ing eyes; then putting his free hand over hers which held his arm he said slowly:

"Why are you so concerned? Why should you care what happens to me?"

His question made her self-conscious and instantly she became embarrassed and shy. She tried to take her hand away, but he held it close.

She longed to turn and run, but it was as if he compelled her against her will to stay.

She knew she must answer him but her voice seemed lost in her throat.

"Tell me, Fleur," Norman said authoritatively.

"I ... can't ..."

"Why not?"

"Because ... I am not sure now it is what you want to ... hear."

"Not sure that I love you?"

"N ... no that's why ... I went away ..."

"My darling—my sweet!"

It was the cry of a man who sees the end of his journey at last and believes that the gates of El Dorado are opening for him.

He swept her into his arms; she felt his heart beating against her own, she felt his arms, strong and virile, holding her breathtakingly close; then her head was against his shoulder and his lips were on hers. Fleur felt them hard, possessive and demanding.

Something warm and wonderful rose within her. She felt as if she was melting into Norman, drawing closer and closer to him. It was so perfect she could not breathe with the loveliness of it.

Then as his kisses became more passionate, almost fierce in their intensity, she felt as if a streak of lightning shot through her, so vivid that it was almost painful and yet an ecstasy she had never known.

It was love—a love that brought with it all that she had longed for and lost in the past, but this time it was part of the Divine.

She felt as if Norman gave her all the beauty she had sought in the Priory but so much more besides—the beauty of the sky, the stars, the whole universe!

He raised his head and looked down at her.

"Now, my precious," he said, and his voice was curiously unsteady, "tell me what I want to hear."

His arms tightened as he went on:

"I want to hear you say it—God knows I want it, more than I've ever wanted anything in my whole life."

Fleur drew in her breath.

"I love . . . you, oh, Norman, I love you . . . be kind to me. I've never felt like this before . . . I'm afraid."

"Afraid?"

"That . . . I shall . . . lose you."

It was true she thought. Before she had always lost everyone she loved and if she lost Norman she would no longer want to go on living.

"You will never lose me, my darling," he said gently. "Like you, I have never felt like this before—I've never been in love until now."

Fleur made a little inarticulate murmur of joy and hid her face against him.

"We'll build a new life together," Norman went on. "Just as when the war is over we'll build a new house. Will you help me?"

Fleur raised her head, her eyes were shining like stars through the irrepressible tears.

"A home big . . . enough for lots of our . . . children . . ." she whispered.

"My precious love!"

Norman was kissing her again until the room whirled round her, and everything vanished except the passionate insistence of his lips.

"How soon will you marry me—tomorrow? The next day?"

She could not believe a man's face could be so transformed by happiness. He looked young and ardent and she knew he was pleading with her.

"As soon as . . . you want . . . me."

She could not say any more, with a sound of triumph, his mouth made her his captive and she knew she could never escape.